Shreds of a Monk's Robe

Tadeusz Chabrowski

Translated from the original Polish

by Albert Juszczak

New York 2001-2009

Bayberry
books

www.bayberrybooks.com

ISBN 978-0-9892133-5-6

Because these wings are no longer wings to fly
But merely vans to beat the air
The air which is now thoroughly small and dry
Smaller and dryer than the will
Teach us to care and not to care
Teach us to sit still.

(fragment)

Ash Wednesday
T.S. Eliot

Dear Mom,

We left the monastery at nine o'clock in the morning in the old Nysa, a van with no windows. The monastery uses it to transport food products and in certain circumstances clerics as well. The driver of the car Mr. Władysław Z., whom I sometimes meet in the monastery courtyard, put in two wooden benches for us to sit on.

At first I did not want to believe that we could all fit into this modest, blue-painted vehicle. In the morning, at breakfast in the refectory, I first met the four new candidates for the noviti-ate. Our guardian, brother Sylwester, also had to go with us. In addition to us, a large sack of potatoes and two smaller ones of buckwheat and flour were loaded into the van.

When the door slammed shut we started to look for a com-fortable place on the hard and unsteady benches. Each of us had to find a handle or a point of support. I sat down on the sack of potatoes. We reacted to the discomfort with humor, directing our attention toward getting to know our fellow travelers.

Brother Sylwester sat in the cab with the driver. When the car started, he opened the window in the dividing wall and started a conversation with us. He reminded us that during the trip, for our safety, we should hold onto the canvas straps attached to the sidewalls. Władysław from Wrocław (the oldest one among us) who sat near the window, peppered him with questions about monastic life.

Brother Sylwester was clearly in a good mood: he started scaring us with getting up early, reciting the breviary in Latin, and the monotony of monastic life. I carefully observed my companions. Staszek K.'s face looked downcast, he blinked his eyes and tried to hide his disappointment. I do not know why he aroused my sympathy. Henry W. reacted more calmly. His protruding ears and shock of stiff hair amused me. Izydor O. from Tarnów had a great desire to join the conversation. But Władysław did not give him that chance. I realized at one point that this discussion might be useful, because every scrap of information about the religious life might come in handy in the near future. The conversation was interrupted when we saw the monastery buildings.

The first impression at the sight of the monastery and the church was depressing. We instantly realized that Leśniów is no Częstochowa, and the monastery clinging to the church was no Jasna Góra. Everything was three quarters smaller, poorer, and less conspicuous. Instead of walls around the monastery - a board fence no longer in peak condition. A dozen fruit trees in the garden, a few rows of tomatoes and vegetables.

At dinner, I had a chance to look the remaining candidates over. Thirteen came from Skałka, from Krakow, the other six from various parts of Poland. For dinner we got barley soup and noodles with cabbage, and an apple for dessert. During leisure after dinner we met a few novices from the previous year and several clerics from Skałka, who came here on vacation. It sounded like the fracas at a church festival. There were low voices, and high, hoarse ones and falsettos. Not one female soprano, not a single ounce of noise coming from the street.

Later that same evening we started the ten-day retreat, led by Father Karol Koproś, the Novice Master.

Kisses and greetings,
Your son

PS. Mom, I wrote this letter with the thought that I'd send it by way of brother Sylwester, who is spending the night here and will be returning to Częstochowa on Monday. I think that will work. Say hello to Dad, Janek, auntie, and Mrs. Krystyna.

Sunday, August 19

The Reverend Novice Master, Karol Koproś, who will be our spiritual guide, impressed us hugely from the start. Tall as a poplar, emaciated, slightly stooped in the shoulders, dressed in the floor-length white robes of the Pauline order, he looked like a phantom that could disappear any moment. During the pre-retreat conference his face looked like the painful face of Christ on the cross.

First impressions are usually the most lasting. I intensify my concentration to remember as much as possible. The Reverend Master begins all of his speeches with an invocation to the Holy Spirit. He kneels on both knees at the altar and humbly asks for the grace of enlightenment, which is necessary to know the truth. He ends it with the sentence:

Speak, Lord, for thy servant is listening.

Then he sits down on a well-worn, portable armchair, shrinks into himself like a snail, closes his eyes and begins speaking. The conference quickly turns into a monologue, a sort of loud contemplation. What reaches us from his barely parted lips is that chaos rules the world, along with perverted justice, people just chase after money, they exude coldness and lack of love of their neighbor. In the dark caves of our souls things happen that we will never unravel without Divine Grace.

The monastery gives everybody the opportunity to listen in on one's inner self. To get to know ourselves as we really are. Those, who first hear the anxiety of their own conscience, will be the first to be rewarded with joy of the heart. But you first have to renounce Satan and wipe every stain of evil off your soul. Next, one has to renounce the world, which always leads unto temptation and favors those who have profaned the faith.

The words of our retreat guide start to circle above our heads, like bees released from their hive.

Monday, August 20
In my thoughts I constantly dwell on the past. In school I ran all over the sports field like a greyhound. Few people could outrun me in the chase after the ball. In the classroom, in the seventh row by the window, I preferred to sit quiet as a bunny. I rarely raised my hand to indicate that I knew the topic being discussed by the teacher, that the spark of knowledge had kindled in my eye. I was gath-

ering strength to once again shine on the playfield.

In the evenings my classmates went on dates with the girls from the Traugutt all-girls' high school. But I went with my mom to the Jasna Góra monastery, for the May devotions and night vigils at the Miraculous Image. The next day they told jokes about red-haired Barbaras, Zofias and Halinas whose breasts were billowing beneath their sweaters. About Elizas, as passionate as cats with long, rust-colored hair, and I with the expression of an ostrich, whose neck is constantly getting longer, made snide faces. As if I knew the subject better that I knew the smell of Siamese cats. I didn't have a clue. I obediently ate blueberries with sugar on top, brought by my aunt Irena or her friend Krystyna, and I cocked my ears to listen to rumors about the Pauline Fathers and their monastic secrets. I probably had a crush on aunt Irena, because I remember that I wanted to please her.

Tuesday, August 21

I feel like writing a letter to my younger brother Janek. He probably feels the burden of loneliness and minor duties at home, which we usually did together.

August 21

Dear Janek,

So far, I'm doing okay. The retreat is nearing completion, and the reverend father's voice has gone hoarse. I dozed through some of the conferences with one eye open, because I'm still not on the same page with getting up so early in the morning. In my spare time I write "little essays" according to the method that Professor Wójcicki drummed into our heads at Henryk Sienkiewicz High School. In those days I played ball with you and never had time to do my homework. Now I have time and an undisturbed calm all around me, so I gladly play the scribe. I wrote letters to my mother, my aunt Irena and Mrs. Krystyna. At first I had a hard time, lots of crumpled paper got tossed into the wastebasket.

Easter Retreats, which were held in St. Mary's Church for the students from Sienkiewicz High School, were nothing compared to what is happening here. It's as if you wanted to compare the flight of a paper helicopter over the city, with a German bomber raid during the war. Four times a day my head gets doused with the hot sand of sentences, red-hot quotes from Scripture and the heroic examples of martyrs, who walked without batting an eye on red-hot coals, or let themselves get cooked in boiling oil. This was the first time I heard about many of these martyrs. Father Karol Koproś has a master's degree in morality and knows how to get inside our souls without using a lock pick. You are so lucky that you can still kick the ball around in the fresh air, blab away until the saliva has dried on your tongue.

On Sunday you will be able to come to Leśniów with Mom and Dad to participate in the frocking ceremony. They're going to shave our heads and drape us in white frocks. I'll have to keep my eyes downcast, my hands hidden under the scapular and I won't be able to make stupid faces, to make you laugh.

Do you still get together with Leszek and Heniek? I did not really tell them where I was going. Maybe they'd laugh? They and their parents drink water from different wells. Do not tell them yet that I'm here. Sometimes I am afraid I won't persevere to the end. I do not know if you know that after one year as a novice you have to take vows of poverty, obedience and chastity. I prefer to solve my problems alone. Sometimes we used to squabble over petty, stupid things, and now that you're not in my life anymore, I find that I really need you.

Big hugs,
Marcin

Thursday, August 23

I think fearfully that I am walking on a narrow footbridge, from which there is no turning back. I do not know whether I will find enough persistence and energy to make it to the end here. I feel like my stomach is shrinking at the thought that in the cloister, everything is totally different. At 5:30 in the morning, the copper sound of the bell knocks everybody out of their sleep. I associate it with war, when air-raid sirens droned like that too, when people were immersed in the best part of their sleep. Then we rush to contemplation, which I still do not know how to deal with. You have to remain in a half-kneeling position for 30 minutes reflecting on matters divine and supernatural, which I still don't have the foggiest idea about.

The very thought of being a monk a few weeks before going to the convent brought me pleasure. I could impress my loved ones and draw attention to myself. But what do I know about this life? I remember when, breathless, I would run into the house from the sports field and came upon my mother's friends, sometimes I learned things about the life of the monks which I would have never been able to invent myself. Each of her friends had a confessor at Jasna Góra. They all related their conversations with the monks. They praised the recommended reading. Some praised Little Theresa of the Infant Jesus, admired the diaries she wrote; others preferred St. John of the Cross or the Great Teresa, the reformer of the Carmelite Order. I wondered even then why the Pauline Fathers recommended Carmelite saints, and not their own? Was is possible that there was no monk among them who had been elevated to the altars? Neither aunt Irena, nor Mrs. Krystyna, nor mother had an answer to this question.

I had the impression that they all wanted me to enter the monastery, and then they would be able to get information from me. When at last after the ninth grade I decided to take that step, they asked me to write letters to them. They wanted to know what the monks eat for lunch and dinner, how many times a month they take a bath. Where they go for walks, what is moral theology and canon law. I looked through their rose-colored glasses at the priests, whom I assisted as an altar boy in the morning at Holy Mass, in the Miraculous Chapel, or in the cool and always humid Basilica. And how could it be otherwise. They knew almost everything about their life, while I saw them as weird phantoms, belonging to another world. In order to know them better I had to join their ranks, don the white robe, shave my head and identify with their ideas and life.

Now that I've got one foot in the monastery, I have to get up with them for morning prayers, recite the breviary in Latin, of which I do not understand a single word, to think about matters that I do not yet understand. I am beginning to hesitate - like a diver who is afraid of the touch of cold water. Whatever happens, however, I have to keep moving forward, step by step, day by day. I have to trust my own impulses, just as I did on the sports field, snatching the ball away from under other players' feet, and waiting for the judge's whistle when somebody fouled me.

Friday, August 24

Before I joined the novitiate aunt Irena strongly urged me to write a diary and letters. Even if only two or three sentences per day. Now I see that it is a good idea. During the retreat, when all are silent, I have to somehow occupy my thoughts, which are usually racing off in different directions like spooked horses. The past cannot be tossed into a trash can like a dead cat. Yet during the conference retreat the Novice Master urges us to do so. God knows that I try to carry out this recommendation. But is it possible to suspend breathing for one or two minutes, or say to oneself: do not think, stop the thread that is now digging a groove into your brain?

Today I went to the chapel, choosing a moment when there was no one in it. I went to the window behind the altar, so I could look at the wonderful statue of Our Lady of Leśniów and earnestly begged her to suggest the thought to me of how I could live in the constant presence of God and not to return to the thoughts of all that is engraved in my memory before coming to the monastery. I promised myself that I would henceforth recite the rosary every day. It seemed to me that she heard me. I returned to my cell with relief in my heart.

August 25

Dear Auntie,

The feeling that I really have no idea how to address you causes me a problem. It became a custom that in the presence of mom and Krystyna, I addressed you as Ma'am, and when we were alone - as Auntie. Often, after returning home from my sports feats on the school's sports field I listened to your hours-long spiritual conversations, understanding one-tenth of what your were saying. I wondered sometimes why your discussions constantly centered on "mystical" subjects. I guessed that you had once diligently studied the books of Saint Teresa of Avila - the great mystic from Spain, and Mrs. Krystyna avidly read religious literature and together with my mom you had subjects for every night of the week.

Thanks to the conversations you had I'll be able to make more rapid contact with my colleagues in the novitiate. I do not know any of them well yet. Immediately after arrival at the monastery we started the retreat. We were forbidden all contact and conversation with our colleagues. We communicate by half-whisper, fragments of sentences, or by writing on scraps of paper. The day here is so organized that there is little time for personal matters.

For now we live in two large halls, sleeping on mattresses stuffed with fresh straw. I do not know whether you will be able to come to my robing, to see me in my white robes. Listening to your conversations I dreamed that one day I would be able to treat you to such a surprise. Reminiscences about Father Eusebius, to whom you used to go for confession, still hang in my mind like a picture of a saint. Also, the figure of Father Honorius, to whom Mrs. Krystyna used to go to confession, is still before my eyes. Your reminiscences of them softened in my imagination like the first snowflakes on November leaves.

I promise myself that after the robbing one of the first books I'll turn to will be the works of Saint Teresa of Avila. I wonder if I will understand something of her "Path of Perfection" and "Interior Castle."

Auntie, please pray for me, and I hope to see you on Sunday. If not, I will pass along a letter through my mother. Best wishes from Marcin, who has already survived seven days in the hermits' monastery.

Marcin

Sunday, August 26

Today, during a solemn Mass. celebrated in the presence of our parents and families before the miraculous statue of Our Lady of Leśniów, under the attentive eye of the Reverend Novice Master Karol Koproś, we were clothed in monastic robes by the Very Reverend Abbot of the monastery in Leśniów Father Anatol Rodwański. Our robes were of white cloth, consisting of four pieces: a tunic to the ankles, a stiff belt at least 9 inches wide, the scapular and a hood over the head, folded back. On the left side attached to the waist a wooden rosary of large black beads. On Saturday evening they cut our hair, and shaved a tonsure on our heads with the diameter of a priest's communion host. As a sign of our monastic baptism we received new names, and our past is to die for the world and us. I, as Marcin – a civilian, athlete, and sinner, must be reborn as Brother Modest, a hermit who will find God in solitude and become like him.

This is a very dry note, which like a rabbit fleeing a fox over marshy wetlands, does not touch the bottom of the terrain that it is fleeing over. There was nothing mentioned in it about the moods that prevailed yesterday among the boys, who's heads were being shaved. Their facial expressions changed from one minute to the next. Władysław from Wrocław went through the most grimaces. Today he received the name of Nepomucen. He was the last to have his hair cut. He was impressed by Henryk's shaved head, who was named Polikarp; his huge protruding ears made him look like an Australian koala bear. Few smiled, because every one knew that in a few minutes he would look like a short-cropped, white-headed Hoopoe Bird. The floor was covered with our hair and it was a grim sight, because everyone seemed to be looking at this battlefield and seeking his own locks of hair. The room grew brighter thanks to our shaved heads. Some tenderly stroked the desolate place on their head, others scratched behind the ear, looked for a way out of the situation, which from moment to moment was becoming increasingly irreversible.

Two colleagues, whose tonsures were cut crookedly in the middle of their heads, had to report to Brother Jack, barber to the Prior, to have them perfected. For this reason the corrected tonsures were a half-inch too big, and both heads gleamed like twin moons in the sky. A trickle of blood appeared on Staszek's head, who was named Melchior. Brother Basil, the volunteer from the seminary high school in Cracow, cut him with the razor so deeply that we had to hastily find alum to skin over the fresh incision. Staszek was crest fallen for the rest of the evening and his struggle not to react in an improper manner was clearly written on his face.

Nevertheless, the evening was gayer than all the others so far; everybody could talk and release the stress that had been accumulating in each one of us. The new names that we were given as a sign that the "old man" was dying in us and a "new one was being born," inspired rather contradictory feelings. First of all these were not commonly known names. It seemed as if someone had hauled them in a dusty casket from the distant past and now tried to surprise those on whom the names were to be bestowed.

During the retreat father Karol quite often referred to this name-changing ceremony as "the new baptism", which would bleach our souls; "the donning of a new dress" before we would be admitted to the "royal wedding". At one point he compared the event to the grafting of wild fruit trees in the spring. Only after tasting the new, refined fruit, would it be possible to recognize just how profound the changes were that had taken place in us.

Monday August 27

My impressions of yesterday's ceremony will be with me for a long time. First of all, hardly anyone of us knows how to walk in a monk's robe. It goes down to the ankles and the bottom is as ample as a parachute. On bending down we automatically stepped on it and lost our balance. To maintain balance, we threw our hands out to the sides, which according to the Reverend Novice Master's instructions should always be hidden beneath the scapular, especially when talking to lay people. When, after the second or third tripping I looked around, almost every one of my colleagues had the bottom of his robe green from contact with grass, or decorated with dark streaks of dust swept up from the floor.

Another sight that entrenched itself in my memory was the families of my colleagues. Almost all were from villages scattered throughout Poland. Many were from Podlasie, probably because the local Pauline monastery has a very active Prior. The second group came from the sub-Carpathian region, mainly from the vicinity of Tarnów, and the third from areas near Warsaw, mainly Ostrołęka. Their exterior appearance strongly emphasized their origin, but my parents, especially my mom, stood out by their tasteful attire and elegant behavior. Father with his fluffy, slightly wavy hair looked like an artist. I was really proud of my parents.

The most distinguished in dress and behavior were the parents of Brother Sophronius, my immediate neighbor in the choir, to whom my monastic fate binds me for the rest of my life. His mother and father arrived in rubber boots, the skin on her face was sun-parched and wrinkled, her hands thickened and destroyed by heavy farm work. Knowing them will help me to better understand their son. The only beautiful adventure, which monastic life has already given him, is his new name - Sophronius, which in my opinion was tinged with ancient Rome and reminded of Petronius from the novel Quo Vadis.

I felt sorry for Brother Longinus, who grew up in an orphanage, and for Brother Nepomucen from Wrocław – no one came to them. Now I had a better idea of our group, which derived from peasant stock and represented whole wheat and rye piety, which I will have to live with closely from this moment in my everyday existence in the monastery.

There was barely two hours of togetherness and talking with our families. Some of us received small gifts, which if they had no practical application, had to be returned or else handed over to the Novice Master. That is how he ended up with some candy, chocolates, flowers and two watches. I got a pair of creaking new shoes from my dad that we had looked at in the Bata store window on Blessed Virgin Mary's Second Avenue in Częstochowa, before I departed for the novitiate. My mother brought me two square-lined notebooks for writing, and letters from Aunt Irena and Mrs. Krystyna. I read both of them and then returned them, explaining that it was better that I not have them on me. I also warned my mother that I would not be able to write many letters, because the Novice Master is not too keen about it. I also handed her my letters - already written - as probably the last. She looked very upset with this news.

I worried about my brother's downcast face. He probably missed my company at home and on the soccer field. We were both very good at kicking the ball. He was impenetrable on defense, I ran like the wind on the left wing, or distributed the ball from my position in the center and often shot goals. Colleagues from the soccer field did not want us to be on the same team, because then our group almost always won. I managed to cheer him up for a moments with these reminiscences. Mom then whispered in my ear:

"Janek feels very lonely without you."

Tuesday, August 28

Yesterday, at an evening of recreation, the Novice Master decided who of us was going to live with whom for then next three months. There would be at least three or four novices in each cell, but never two. I found myself in cell No. 23, and my comrades were Brothers Leon and

Felix. Leon has a great appetite, he's quite stout, but has an exceptionally cheerful disposition and it's hard to upset him. He reminds me of a village headman, who used to be well off and who still wants to impress others.

Felix, with dark blond hair and a gentle disposition, is sometimes as nervous as the winter Tit bird. His pleasant voice brightens us up, when he hums a happy song. We six, who were the last to sign up for the novitiate, were mixed in with the candidates from the seminary high school. This will help us quickly integrate with their group.

In the cell there is room for three beds, three chairs, a stool with a wash basin, a water pitcher and a soap dish. When compared to the cave of St. Paul the First Hermit, this is the luxury of a Białystok hotel. The Novice Master reminded us that Paul used a stone for his pillow, he wore a dress made of woven palm leaves, and his sole nourishment was half a loaf of bread brought by a raven and pure spring water.

We undress for sleep with the light out.

Wednesday, August 29

Today after breakfast, the Novice Master announced that we could report to him to get books for spiritual reading. I went to him first, thinking that I'd have more choice. However, this had no greater significance. The Reverend Father had a prepared list of titles in front of him and allocated them according to the sequence in which each of us was admitted to the Order. I was four-teenth, and that is probably why I received the second volume of the "Lives of the Saints" by the Rev. Piotr Skarga.

At first I could not understand how such a sequence was determined. One of the novices, Brother Leo, from the Cracow seminary high school group, explained it to me as follows: Brother Basil is a senior in our group, because he was the first to report to the Order. I am the ninth, and you, Brother, are fourteenth after Brother Sophronius, who was the last in our seminary high school. Age is not taken into account. When we finish the novitiate, and take our vows, we will become part of the statistical numeration of the entire Order, with regard to the sequence that now applies.

At two o'clock the bell announced that it was time for spiritual reading. After opening the leather bound second volume of **Lives of the Saints** I was overcome by enormous astonishment. The book was printed in Cracow in 1899. As a rare book it should have been serenely standing on a bookshelf, and my sweaty fingers should not have been touching it. My eyes parsed its yellowed, crumbling pages with reverence and respect.

The volume treated of three months: April took up 358 pages, May 431 pages and June 424. I guessed that the Novice Master had a specific goal in mind when he gave me the volume. I started to delicately turn the pages, looking for my patron saint. Indeed, under the date of June 15, three martyrs were described: Wit, Modest and Kresencja.

The main hero of the story was St. Wit, a twelve-year boy raised by his mother in ardent faith in Christ. His father, a pagan, became afraid of the threats of the emperor Diocletian, who forced his subjects to offer sacrifices to the gods of Rome. Despite stern warnings from his father and threats of painful punishment from the emperor's enforcers, the young follower of Christ did not let himself be persuaded to worship foreign gods. As a sign that Christ remembered the brave boy, God "withered the hands of the executioners."

The frightened father tried to tempt his son to try a dissolute life of music, dance and the society of frivolous women. The young man prayed: "Lord, don't let me get stuck in these snares, let this devil be disgraced." His father did not back down, and Wit's stubbornness did not decline. Then Modest, Wit's guardian from birth, decided that he, Wit and his nurse Kresencja ought to leave, to disappear from before his father's and the executioners' eyes.

By divine dispensation they landed near the river Syler. There Wit started talking about Christ, performed many miracles, and urged the local population to believe in Christ. Diocletian quickly learned about this activity. He ordered Wit, Modest and Kresencja to be stretched with various irons in the torture chamber and to be subjected to a multiplicity of other tortures. As they were dying a "great earthquake toppled many of the pagan temples."

Piotr Skarga's language made a huge impression on me; it was so different from what I had been used to in school ... The description of tortures and miracles merged with the reality of life as it was then. Saint Modest, on whom I was to model myself, was the servant of a great miracle-worker and apostle. He played the role of a guardian, he never played the main role, but he persevered to the end at the side of the martyr. I began to suspect that a similar role ought to be mine as well in my monastic life.

Thursday, August 30

Instead of reading a short sermon meant for "The Day of the Holy Angels, especially the supreme Michael", I succumbed to the temptation of a bibliophile. I admired the book itself more than the contents, with which I was supposed to feed my soul. The book covered the Church's third quarter, that is, the biographies of saints from July 1 and "The Life of Samson", until September 30, and "The Life of St. Jerome." The Reverend Piotr Skarga wrote his work in 1579. He furnished it with a lengthy introduction that discusses the spiritual benefits to be achieved by reading the lives of the saints of the Old and New Order. He also discussed the recommendations given to us in the New Testament and by the Fathers of the Church.

The copy, which I tenderly stroked with my fingers, had very yellowed pages; here and there one could see single words or whole sentences underlined. I was surprised that it was still in circulation, and not in a glass display case. I handled it as one would handle a patient with asthma. The work was printed in 1899 in A. Koziański's printing press in Cracow.

I began with the very colorful biography of St. Wenceslaus, which was the subject of yesterday evening's breviary recitation. His grandmother Ludmiła raised him, a woman of great integrity and wisdom. His mother Dragomira, who took care of his younger brother Bolesław, did not have similar virtues. As a result of her palace intrigues the grandmother was strangled. Despite this, Wenceslaus became the King of Bohemia and "as a second David, began all his affairs with consideration of God." While holding such high office he did not fail to mortify his flesh: "At night, when nobody saw him, he walked to church with his bare feet, and also in the winter when it was bitterly cold and also when it was snowing." He was a valiant king, who won the recognition of the emperor, who "gave him the hand of St. Wit the Martyr, a great treasure of a gift." Unfortunately, the brutal palace intrigues and his mother, "irreligious and bowing to the devil," and the jealous brother grasping for power led to the abject murder of Wenceslaus. He lived from about 907 to 935 A.D.

Friday, September 1
During a morning conference on the life of ascetic monks, the Reverend Novice Master introduced us to a subject that I knew little about before entering the novitiate. One of my mother's friends had mentioned discipline, that is, the physical mortification of one's own body on Fridays, but my vigilance apparently did not attach any im-

portance to this subject.

The conference began differently than all the previous ones. The Reverend Father came with a cardboard box, which he did not open until the end of the lecture. He told how formerly monks in monasteries mortified their bodies with fasting, night vigils and cruel rebuke - with rods of rose thorn, waxed leather straps or a cord made of twisted rope. My colleague's faces became slightly overcast. At Brother Longinus' question as to why monks are to mortify their body like that, the Novice Master explained:

"Mortification of the flesh is a virtue. It signifies moral victory over oneself and the monk's religious attitude toward sin. The monk by mortifying his body strikes a balance between good and evil. He knocks the instrument of violence out of the devil's hands. He stands on the side of the good spirits who are trying to bring about order in the world, justice and the fear of God."

After the conference we were able to walk up to the box and choose a whip. Some were with a handle, others without, but firmly looped at the base. It turned out later that those with a handle were more effective and one could severely lash one's body with them. In the evening, after switching off the light, we could try the usefulness of an instrument of penance on ourselves. The first contact was painful; no one seemed to realize that the body can be so sensitive. One had to control the hits and the tension of the skin.

In the stream of moonlight I observed the barely visible silhouette of Brother Leo. Brother Felix, of a slighter build, was less visible. The first lashes were bold; the next ones grew successively milder. After five or six hits, each one of us hastily slipped under the covers. There was plenty to contemplate for the next hour.

I finally understood why silence is an important element in monastic life. The first manifestations of fear, cowardice and pain were better off buried deep under the skin. It was better not to feel the shrinking of one's body into itself. Let the ears not hear the gasp of the lips. Let the head not know that the soles of our feet are bleeding.

Saturday, September 2
I looked through the window at the wet, gray walls. A bit of grass is growing two floors below in the square cloister garden, but has a very dull shade of green. The sun does not penetrate there. In the gutter on the opposite side two sparrows are bathing in the rainwater and preening their feathers. They look happy. Too bad that we can not treat our eyes to views of a garden, watch flowers and trees bloom, breathe in the air, in which one can still hear the twitter of the Thrush or Titmouse. Or try to catch the inaudible flutter of the white cabbage butterfly's wings.

The supervisors proceed from the assumption that the less views for the eyes, the less the temptations for body and mind. I am not particularly sad on this count. It may be that in the near future, I will stop counting the hours that still remain to the end of the day and week. And I won't succumb to the senseless doubts that I won't be able to endure to the end within these walls.

If I were now to give in to such doubts, then my mother, Aunt Irena, my neighbors and colleagues would become my judges. Their current sympathy would change to contempt. Everybody is expecting more than I can deliver. In utter isolation, I can only ask God that each successive day be easier and cut less at my unprotected interior.

Sunday, September 3

I should write a letter to Mrs. Krystyna, a close friend of my mother and Aunt Irena. Both were part of our family. Something serious would have had to happen for them not to visit in the evening. Plump Mrs. Krystyna, with long fingers and a beautiful complexion, always smiling, was often present in my thoughts.

September 3

Dear Mrs. Krystyna,

Thank you for the greetings sent by mama. She reminded me of my promise to write letters to you. I did not fulfill my promise, because we have a very tight schedule of assignments planned for each day. Our founders thought that monasteries are for angels with astral souls, without passions and emotions, and not for people as insignificant as me. I do not know if I will find a place for myself here. For now, like a lost sparrow I wander around the corridors and try to flap my imaginary wings. I do not know how long my strength will last.

During our spiritual retreat we have already heard nearly 30 conferences, lasting from 45 minutes to an hour. We daily recite the litany to the Guardian Angels, we walk the Way of the Cross. Each day we recite the Prime and Terce from the Latin Breviary, Vespers in the afternoon and the Matutinum in the evening. We have time set aside for spiritual reading. During meals we have read to us "The Life of St. Gabriel of the Blessed Mother of Sorrows." In the evening before going to sleep we do a detailed examination of conscience, according to the questions prepared by our spiritual guide. After all these prayers and exercises we go to our cells to sleep.

In enumerating the various activities I did not mention the morning Mass with which everything begins, Holy Communion and Thanksgiving. That after all these spiritual exercises I do not radiate light like a firefly, you would have to blame my balky nature ...

Dear Mrs. Krystyna, I never had any personal conversations with you. But I knew that you have extensive knowledge of subjects related to spiritual life and Catholic literature. I sensed that you are married, but you never mentioned your husband. With my mother and aunt Irena you often discussed such topics as purity, lofty ideals and sacrifices. You knew the biographies of many saints better than Sienkiewicz or Żeromski. Over the past three years I existed on the margins of your garden, lit up with the sun of asceticism. The dew of your sympathy helped me cherish the dream of a vocation in my heart.

I served at Mass for all of your confessors. Sometimes I delivered envelopes with your confidential messages or brought from them letters addressed on a typewriter. Slowly, everyone got used to seeing me as a messenger who delivers news. With time every messenger grows wings. I also managed to fly from the tiny streets around Jasna Góra to Leśniów, from the Sparks sports field in Częstochowa to the twelve-yard wide and long monastic patio enclosed by a monastery wall.

Respectfully yours,
Brother Modest

Monday, September 4

In the morning, without haste, as if I were writing down a dictation, I penned the first poem in my life ... I hope – it's a poem:

Patio

A modest retreat enclosed by a square wall,
the sun peers in once a day at noon,
birds lurk in the branches of a tree,
to listen to the monks' Gregorian melodies,
they already know the Sext and None by heart.

Sometimes brother Macarius carries something out in a
frying pan
for the cat who takes care that the mice do not enter

the cloister and tempt the monks to sin;
the crackling crunch of tiny bones is not surprising,
the mice for sure will go to heaven.

At the edge of the night all sorts of rustling can be heard,
Brothers throw orange peels out the windows,
sometimes serious sins for which they did not get
absolution, sometimes dreams
that rush into an uncertain twilight.

In winter, when there's a dusting of snow, it is white,
as soon as the dawn lights up
angels fly in to sing Matins and Vespers,
then the stomping of the Three Kings is heard,
As they run on Christmas Day to Bethlehem.

I was at the Novice Master's. Voluntary conversations with him are highly recommended. You have to open your soul to him, confess the trip-ups, absurdities and irregularities. He may suggest something practical; discover where meanness or disease have nestled in the soul. I told him that I breathe the best on paper, when I write letters to my mother, aunt and brother, though I don't always have the desire to send them to recipients. However, my greatest desire is to establish a correspondence with my cousin, sister Florencja, who preceded me to the novitiate by three months. She lives in the congregation of Samaritan Benedictine Sisters of the Cross of Christ in Niegów near Warsaw.

The Novice Master was of the opinion that such a spiritual intercourse with a woman can lead to impure thoughts and awaken dreams that I won't be able to deal with in the not too distant future. I mentioned to him that we lived together, and my mother and my aunt fed us the same pious recommendations for many months. Nonetheless the Reverend Novice Master looked at me with indulgent pity. A minute before leaving my head was spinning with the advice that he stuffed into my ears in an emphatic whisper. For the first time his ascetic admonitions ceased being more real to me than the breath of truth itself.

I also realized that my naive sincerity could turn against me. Probably that is why fools never become saints.

Tuesday, September 5
After yesterday's conversation with the Novice Master, I can't put myself together. I wanted to thank my mother, father and brother for their visit. Their arrival assured me that they are still around, just an hour's drive away by bus. At any troublesome moment I can join them and be part of the family. Now I know that writing letters is not advisable. And if I write a letter, I won't be able to send it. I do not have money for a stamp. I can only write for my desk drawer.

Dear Ones,

I feel much calmer after your visit. All those murky suspicions, that my future is uncertain – have become much milder. The fact that I could meet with you once again that you didn't fly out of my world forever, grounded me more securely in reality. I felt sorry that my dad spent so much money on the shoes. They squeak when I walk, and sometimes I feel embarrassed to go in them to the chapel.

Dad, you looked great, like Paderewski with that thick shock of hair. My colleagues asked me if you are an artist. I nodded proudly. Besides, there was no inconsistency in that. I remember your album with sketched caricatures of famous people, vases, flowers, and birds' heads faithfully copied from botanical books and colored with pastels. You concealed that album from us, because it also contained portraits of mom and her friends in various hats and bathing suits. Bold dedications beneath the pictures proved that they all had a nice and cheerful time.

I also remember Dad, your work in the churches: the restored ceiling in the choir at the Basilica of Jasna Góra, renovated polychromes in the parish church of St. Barbara, intricately carved patterns in card stock to reproduce the symbols of the Eucharist - IHS. Yes, Dad, you really are and always will be an artist for me, despite the fact that immediately after the war you had to paint houses and large school classrooms. It is strange that all this is only now rising to the surface of my memories.

Janek! You too looked handsome in that sweater with

navy blue splotches. Perhaps you just had a tad of a frown on your face. You complained that your friends were tormenting you with questions about me. Don't worry - a bit more and they will be used to the fact that you have a brother in the novitiate.

Mom, you treated me to a big surprise with the arrival of Rysiek P.'s mother. With that hat, not much smaller than our garden, she attracted almost everybody's attention. We were still in the choir, and I already knew she was in the church because of the fragrance of her lavender perfume. It was good that she appeared alone, without Rysiek. I would not have been able to bear any more joy of her creation. During the meeting she clattered her tongue like a tin drum. If she had stayed for just one night in the monastery, by morning half of the residents would have to be transported to the nut house.

Mom, you looked beautiful and young in that two-piece suit the color of ripe peaches. The fact that I'm here in this white robe I owe to your gentle persistence. I hope that I don't disappoint you.

Warm hugs for All
Marcin

Wednesday, September 6

I had a spate of bad luck. Yesterday during the walk from the chapel to the refectory I stepped on Brother Longinus' shoelace. His shoe fell off and we both lurched out of line. He was very upset and pinched my cheek. I did not know how to behave. At dinner I felt my skin burn. Brother

Longinus, when I looked furtively at him, was biting his lip, and blinked an eye at me, as if nothing had happened.

During the recreation period I learned from Brother Luke that Brother Longinus is an illegitimate child and grew up in an orphanage. My anger quickly evolved into compassion. I decided to establish closer contact with him.

Friday, September 8
My thoughts wandered in the darkness well into the middle of the night. I was looking for words, with which I could describe my place in the monastery. I realized that my "self" is just a drop of water in the belly of a whale. It is becoming part of a whole that has 27 heads, 54 feet gliding over the floor and the same number of hands swaying in a slow procession around the main aisle of the church. This collective body is able (with me or without me) to recite psalms in Latin in a monotonous voice, sing Gregorian chants during mass and vespers, breathe with an enormous lung that sucks the air out of the chancel and choir; it blows out carbon dioxide that flies and spiders devour, and every Friday it beats its breast with a huge fist.

I am tormented by anxiety even when I sleep. A month ago I was still the son of Edmund Kołacz, a tenant in a small brick apartment house, a ninth grader at the Henryk Sienkiewicz High School, the left guard on the Sparks junior soccer team. In the monastery I am becoming a faint shadow. A stain on the wall, which cannot be included in a game, which can wash out at any time.

I can forgive myself everything, except suddenly descending into sluggishness.

Sunday, September 10
Early in the morning I had to go to the toilet. I strained my ears to hear how the walls breathe; I even thought that I heard the rustle of air in the corridor. Drops of water dripping from the faucet were as heavy as milk cans. I stood in the emptiness and waited. The absence of everything suddenly became unbearable.

After some time drowsiness as gentle as the blueness on the little statue of the Blessed Virgin Mary in the chapel, began to close my eyes. All the feathers that had been bristling just a moment before now began to settle in around the frozen body. For a moment I felt as if I were an angel in a snow-white surplice that can wait standing by the wall for half of eternity.

Tuesday, September 12
I write letters to my mother, and immediately destroy them. I am unable to choose the right words. It only now occurs to me that the Novice Master is introducing a new language in the novitiate, using words in such a way that when I try to use them again, they don't fit anything. On the one hand, I try to accept the values presented by him, to understand what the inner life is all about;

on the other hand I still do not comprehend what I need to change in myself to build this new life. I would like to show my mother that I already understand something of this new language, but my words trip over each other, and are not credible.

September 12

Dear Mom,

I have already written a few letters to you, but I destroyed them. The Reverend Novice Master tells us that the devil is constantly milling about and sets traps for the unprepared. By indulging myself in writing on paper, I give him a chance to peek into my soul. He for sure knows how to read, just as he knows how to twist violet strings into hangman's ropes for sinners. At home I could talk about everything with you. Together with aunt Irena you were able to come up with good advice for everything. Besides, what kind of troubles did I have then? Aunt was able to find a quotation from the books of St. Teresa of Avila for every problem, or some kind of encouragement for godly living. Here I have even more of these stimuli, but they don't all penetrate my skin.

Mom, I am struggling with my thoughts and myself. I miss you and I miss home, although I should not write about it. At home I could have fun on the sports field and I was able to fall into deep sleep at once. Here the monastery walls are silent day and night. The silence seems so overwhelming that one's eardrums could burst from it.

If suddenly, in the dim light of these corridors, I found him alone with Jesus, I would for sure get scared of his loud breathing. Just like Moses, two horns would sprout on my forehead from fear. Thus far, I did not much believe in the physical presence of the devil. I treated thoughts of him as a postscript in the catechism, spilled all over in fine print.

Reverend Father the Novice Master talks about him in away so strange that new specters and scarecrows multiply in my imagination. In many biographies of saints, he appears like a piece of furniture thrown onto a garbage pile, which – who knows how – someone keeps bringing back home and abandoning in a dark corner.

Mom, do not deduce any gloomy thoughts from this letter. I only write about what is sometimes being said here. In Dad's fairy tales the devil appeared too, but as the lame Boruta. Do not reply to this letter. The Novice Master reads our correspondence and I do not want him to know that such misleading thoughts still buzz inside my head. He may think that I want to cry in your lap.

God probably knows better how to avoid errors. He does not need to frighten people with the devil.

Marcin

Thursday, September 14
Today, for the first time we took a long walk outside the monastery with the Novice Master. This was a new experience for us, but also a direct interaction with

nature. The weather was good, the sun, not covered by any clouds, delightedly sought out our pale faces and hands. The wind tugged at our robes at will, as if guessing that we were hungry for open space and fresh air.

Everybody's faces became cheerful, one could blab at will, without lowering one's voice. We walked in threes and twos – at will. Sometimes like geese, in single file, when we had to walk between fields of wheat or potatoes.

The Novice Master's demeanor was also less solemn. He did not weigh every word down to the ounce. He reacted to jokes and gave the impression that he was in a good mood. It was probably important to him that outside, in relative freedom, each of us was himself, not concealed behind a pious facial expression.

The thirteen from the seminary high school knew each other well, and led the pack. From our group the freest were Brothers Longinus from the orphanage and Nepomuk, who ventured out on this walk in shining patent leather shoes. Brother Fabian also brimmed with jokes a la Falstaff and entertained everyone. The Novice Master, around whom we all sat down, felt like Jesus among his apostles.

At first we couldn't figure out what to do with our scapulars and hoods. Some, while walking flipped them onto their right arm, others hitched their tunics up quite high, so as not to get them dirty. Brother Fabian was the first to risk taking his hood and scapular off his arms. Drops of sweat beaded up on his forehead. It turned out that this solution was not possible - not now, when you are a novice, and wearing a robe from morning to night is one of the main requirements. On this occasion the Father Magister reminded us that a good novice should not only endure any discomforts of the day, but also look for them. That is the only way to gain true perfection.

Then thermos bottles with a very diluted rhubarb and apple compote were taken out of a backpack. Some rye flour chips appeared out of nowhere, which the cook sometimes bakes when he makes egg drop dumplings for supper. Returning to the monastery the Novice Master chose another route. We walked single file between the fields, saying the rosary aloud all the while. At one point I noticed that we were making an unnecessary turn, lengthening the route. It turned out that the Novice Master, leading our group, noticed a woman on the road with brushwood on her back, heading toward the village. And probably to spare us temptations, he lengthened the route by about half a kilometer.

It was a really successful day. I got to know Brother Leo better, with whom I live now. I talked with Brothers Mark and Arsenius, they told me many interesting stories about the seminary high school. I learned that Brother Felix and Brother Mark are from Radom, attended the same school and after the retreat in the parish, led by Father Piotr, a Pauline, they signed up for the seminary high school.

I think we all had a sound and healthy sleep that night.

Sunday, September 16

At the novitiate it is sometimes difficult to distinguish Sunday from an ordinary day. After lunch we went to the garden for an hour of recreation. The sun scorched our cheeks and necks; we absorbed the last of the summer with our nostrils. I envied the wrens their flights without borders, the flapping of their wings against the air.

On the other side of the fence boys were kicking a ball around. I listened to their laughter and shouts. My beautifully designed purpose in life suddenly became very unimportant. I desired to bury myself in the hustle and bustle of the street, in the hubbub of the stand owners next to the Jasna Góra monastery, the noise of students running out of school after classes. Life is one big meditation. We ourselves don't know what we want.

Brother Leo, with whom I was walking, was also outside the fence in his thoughts. Suddenly the ball fell into the garden. Both of us, like unleashed greyhounds, ran in its direction. My companion overtook me, and with a sure shot off his right foot he kicked the ball towards the players. He got applause. The rest of our conversation rolled on smoothly, mostly oscillating around our sports exploits in school and on the sports field.

After returning from the recreation period we had some free time. I most often use those moments to write letters or my diary. From thoughts scattered throughout the day, I try to write down those that may have some value for me. Often, the pen is more obedient to me than my tongue. In this way I compensate for my absence in all those places where I used to be, or where I would like to be now.

Monday, September 17

I received a letter from aunt Justyna, who is a gardener with the Samaritan Sisters. It's my mother's elder sister, to whom my mother is very attached. Despite this, my mother does not like it when, during her visit, Justyna moves mother's pots around on the stove, or advises her, what to do with her personal life.

September 12

Dear Marcin,

I was in Częstochowa for two days to visit your mom and to pray before the image of Our Lady of Jasna Góra. I am glad that you're in the novitiate already, under the good care of your Novice Master and are trying to find God in the environment of a monastic family. Sister Florencja asked me to greet you. She is in a novitiate, so she probably will not have much time to write. She has to learn a lot, fill herself with the spirit of the congregation and adapt to the difficult work with handicapped children, which our congregation does because of the founder's directive.

In our congregation the novitiate lasts two years. We do not have to study philosophy and theology like seminarians preparing for the priesthood. On the other hand the basics, the fundamentals of the inner life must be very solid in our sisters. Dil-

igent work, prayer and charity are our main postulates. Reading the biographies of great saints is of great importance in preparing for charity work. We need to have a lot of patience, and tenacious willpower, so the work does not discourage us.

I think that being a monk in a closed convent can sometimes be easier than nursing the sick with impaired minds. In keeping cripples alive, God tests our capacity for mutual assistance.

After two months of the novitiate you can probably already distinguish a surplice from a Bishop's cape?

I hope that the Novice Master urges you to make a lot of effort to master the defects of your character, according to the saying about the shell that whatever it became saturated with in its youth, it smacks of in old age. Instead of dealing with the writings of some fourth century Egyptian monk, my dear cousin, engage yourself in real work: daily recitation of your breviary, fasting three times a week, lashing the body every Friday and monastic focus. I do not think I'll have to repeat this when we see each other when you celebrate your first mass in a few years.

If, after these remarks you are not offended, please - from time to time, pray for me, because you in the contemplative convents certainly know how to pray better than we, sisters of the female congregations, exhausted by manual labor, and not so expert in matters of theology. For years, I have been commending you to God in my prayers, and now you have come even closer to me, because you chose the path on which I'm trying to save my soul.

Be with God!

Sister Justyna Notek,
Samaritan Benedictine of the Cross of Christ

My aunt's recommendations were no healing balm that could be massaged into the wounds of the lonely novice. It seems to me on that paper my aunt is trying to play the prioress a bit. Normally, as I remember, she was much nicer. I spent three consecutive holidays under her care. After we had finished our school year my mother would send us to Niegów, to help in the garden, but also to accustom me to monastic life, to have me serve at mass with the chaplain, and to be under the watchful eye of her older sister.

Tuesday, September 18

Today at breakfast I pushed my coffee cup with my elbow onto the floor. The Brother Cook was very much worried about it. He said that maybe something bad would yet happen, because misfortune comes in pairs. Actually, I violated the virtue of poverty. The broken cup cannot be glued back together. Hermits in their caves took great care of their hand-fashioned clay dishes.

I do not know why, I started to blame the devil for this. I thought - if the devil was more visible, I would be able to nail him to the wall in the refectory. Let all abomination drip out of him like dark beet juice.

The next instant I pounded my chest. How could I admit such an idea into my head? Why dump everything on the devil, it was I who was clumsy and distracted. And besides, every creature is part of God's plan. You cannot trample a flower that grows on the path, or a snail, which leisurely crawls along it. The commandment "You shall not kill" is just as important as the proscription "You shall not commit adultery" and "Do not steal." It turns out that I am still very raw material for a monk.

Wednesday, September 19

The Novice Master gave me an opened letter from my religion teacher. Apparently, he read it carefully, because he did not have any additional questions. But his facial expression was none too pleased. I'm getting used to reprimands given by a hand gesture, a puckered face, or an insincere smile.

September 15

Dear Brother Modest (Marcin)!

I received your letter through your mother. I was very touched by it. Thank you for your trust and sincerity, which came through in every word. Allow me, however, to continue addressing you by name, as I did in the past few years. And I would also prefer that you address me as you used to. I do not think that a month's stay in the monastery has inclined you to perceive me differently.

As you know, for years I have been helping the pastor of St. Joseph's Parish in Gnaszyn to prepare children for their First

Communion. If times were different, I could successfully teach religion in high school. Unfortunately, the emancipation of women in civilian life and in the Church is proceeding in very small steps. Nor do I know how it happened that in your eyes I was once a married woman. This is wonderfully incorrect information. I do not have to seek a divorce to feel free again.

The experiences of a novice that you described are the modest beginning of a difficult road that your mind, heart and body will have to travel. Since ancient times, fear of faith has been great. Still, in the conflict of spiritual and secular aspirations, faith alone can dictate the correct solutions. I do not want to sound too loud in this letter. Your spiritual guide will have much more to say. He is guided by the lofty goal of forming young personalities for life in the monastery, showing the shortest route to salvation. In preparing children for their First Communion, I always pray that some of them find their way to the serenity of the monastery.

During our "tea" meetings at your mother's house you are now the object of our spiritual concerns. Your letters fire up our curiosity. So write, write at all cost. It doesn't matter if it will be thirty lines, fifteen or five. Words are the photograph of your interior. During the entire year you will have the unique opportunity to enrich your interior, decorate it like the chapel of the Blessed Mother of Jasna Góra with offerings of your renunciations and prayers. We will accompany you spiritually with our sisterly care.

With best wishes of persevering effort
Krystyna, religion teacher

This letter has great value for me. On those three pages the nice religious teacher told me more about herself than I could find out about her over the last several months. Maybe because I had listened bashfully, without full attention, to everything the ladies visiting my mother were talking about. Now all their conversations are coming back to me and like seeds after a long winter they are sprouting in me.

September 19

My Dear Religion Teacher,

I thought all afternoon how to react to your letter. You poured a bucket of cold water on me. I had been needlessly hiding behind a screen of shyness. In the chapel, in front of the tabernacle, I was embarrassed at the blush on my cheeks. Eyes that cannot differentiate the better from the worse. By calling you "Mrs." in the letter I thought that I would build a wall that would fence me off from you as a woman, so that my monastic purity would be safe. Thinking in categories of the flesh I began to draw false conclusions.

Meanwhile what connects me to you is something very personal. It makes for the beauty of our several year old acquaintance. By addressing you too formally, I gave the impression that I am angry with you, that some sort of misunderstanding had arisen between us, which you know nothing about, and the lack of tact on my part imputes a false judgment. I suppose that I will still be making such errors many times. Sometimes I repeat words that I heard five minutes before at a conference.

I would like to kiss your hand as I used to and to ask you to disperse the gloom above my head.

Brother Modest, i.e. Mr. Modesty

September 13

Dear Marcin,

I found out from Zdzich Z. that you went to a monastery. A brick must have fallen on your head. I cannot imagine a more real world than the one a sportsman has on the sports field. And you were good in kicking the ball, maybe the best of us all. Whoever had you on their team did not have to worry about making goals. And suddenly our well-oiled "machine" (as we used to call you) allowed itself to be lead to a monastery. Zdzich and I were shaking our heads in disbelief.

Maybe it's true that everybody's a lunatic and chooses whatever he dreams up. But you didn't have to hurry, one makes choices after graduation.

We wish you a lot of luck and as short a stay in the monastery as possible.

Leszek K.

P.S. Write when you get bored of life in the monastery, we'll come and pick you up.

Leszek Kulesza's letter is sincere, but really wounds my insides. We lived in the same building, attended the same school. We withheld no secrets from each other. But now I see, that despite everything, we were nurturing two different personalities inside. He was hurt that I didn't tell him the secret of my life. He probably would have reacted differently. But I didn't have enough strength to open myself up to my friend's jokes. I copped out.

September 19

Dear Marcin,

Lucynka S. told me that you took off for the Brothers of St. Paul. I would have never guessed that about you. You did not have your intentions engraved on your forehead. Too bad that you aren't together with us now in tenth grade. Tomek Pośpiech of Sosnowiec joined us, he is a terrific basketball player, and he's more than 6 feet tall. He looks like he's got a great future. Mrs. Stefania Szostek, the mathematician, is on maternity leave. She's not coming back until December. The biologist, Piotr Wisłocki, is substituting for her. He does the lessons straight out of the textbook and is somewhat boring. You know him well, anyhow, what more can I tell you.

When it comes to soccer, we will miss you. Your friends talk about you a lot. I hope they'll let you come home for Christmas, and then we'll be able to talk. Greetings from Lucynka, her brother Stefan and of course big hugs from me and my mother, who also sends you her best.

Yours always,
Zygmunt H.

Zygmunt hasn't changed a bit, I can always count on him, but will I ever need him? Our paths have already diverged. If he were now next to me, I wouldn't have a pouting face for sure. He always radiated energy and warmth like an Icelandic geyser.

Thursday, September 20

I had a very strange dream today: as if I were still living with my parents on 38 St. Roch Street, when our apartment was located between the two apartments of Mr. and Mrs. Szomański. The professor's younger daughter, Jadwiga, practiced her violin in the same room in which her father gave lessons to his students. The composition by Szymanowski that she was playing now was so beautiful, that I opened the door slightly out of curiosity, so I could hear it in even the slightest nuance. I also wanted to see how it was possible to create such beautiful music with the help of a bow made of horsehair and an appropriately shaped wooden box. A melody that awakens emotions excites the senses and inebriates with a tone that vibrates in the air.

After some time I realized that the young female violinist was stark naked, like Mother Eve in paradise. But the desire to listen to the melody was so strong that her nakedness did not actually excite my imagination. Only when the fingers of her left hand started moving more and more quickly along the strings, when her right hand guiding the bow started changing positions with lightning speed, to rise and fall, pressing the swath of horse hair to the strings, to fuse with the instrument and the melody, I then felt that all that vibrating of the air was moving over onto me, and that I felt sensual delight in every cell of my body. I didn't even notice when Jadwiga walked up to me and began drawing the bow across my neck, my elbows and under my knees. I woke up with a scream. My night clothes were all wet, and the remnants of the experienced physical joy still shook my body.

I really didn't know what to do with myself. Why so much joy during sleep and not while awake? Who was directing all of this? Was this a gift from heaven, or a run of the mill trap by Satan trying to smear my soul and body with sin? It bothered me all day long. I dragged my feet as if they were made of lead. I had thought that in the monastery I would be swimming in God's grace like a fish in a mountain stream. And here my own underbelly was refusing to obey. As if it had forgotten that after having received the monk's robes I had told it firmly and unequivocally: from now on no wild surprises, not now and not in this place.

I had to calm my mind with these jottings. I can't approach Father Walerian, my confessor, with this chaos in my head. The old man, due to his obesity, gets emotional about every aberration. After hearing what had happened to me at night, he will feel as if the stones were cracking up again in his liver. I feel sorry for him, because he has goodness in his eyes, compassion and great fear, which can change into terror at any moment.

Friday, September 21

At the afternoon ascetic conference the Novice Master spoke about how talkativeness, lack of respect for the word, can wreak havoc with our interior. He admonished us to refrain from talkativeness and unnecessary words every Friday. The best thing is to maintain silence all day long.

At first I couldn't quite understand why a thought expressed out loud could turn out to be a defect, and an unrevealed thought be a virtue. I had always thought that the gift of speech is the most magnificent distinction that God had gifted Man with. Maybe monkeys are smart, can show tender feelings, take care of their young, but you couldn't put together even a five-page dictionary from their squeaks. Dogs bark too, to warn us of danger, wag their tales in a friendly way in greeting, but they too are dumb.

This coming Friday I will try to adjust to the Novice Master's recommendation. I will see what benefits my soul will derive from this. I suspect that following one's thoughts in the quiet of the cloister may prove more interesting than blabbing about nothing, or next to nothing. I never have enough time to complete my notes. Now every Friday I will be able to get rid of the backlog.

The final sentence of the conference decidedly did not sound banal: "Flies did not fall into St. Paul the hermit's mouth, because he had no one to open it to."

Friday, September 28

I irritated a few of my colleagues today because I tried to maintain silence all day. I talked to them in sign language, and when necessary – I wrote the words down on paper with a pencil. They drew circles on my forehead. A pouting Brother Felix sputtered saliva like a mole after it lifts its head above a puddle, when I tried to explain to him, while washing up in the morning, that our soap had gone soft overnight in the soap dish. Brother Leo acknowledged my oddity with a smile and instead of washing in the wash bowl, he dipped two fingers in the toothbrush cup and wiped his eyelids with them.

During my spiritual reading of Reverend Piotr Skarga's "The Lives of the Saints" I looked for some sort of appropriate affirmation of the weirdness that I had begun to practice today. Even though, at the Novice Master's recommendation, I held my tongue, I wanted to have factual proof for tomorrow that I wasn't doing something stupid. But that Jesuit priest preferred to popularize the lives of martyrs, Roman notables, famous court beauties, who suddenly decided to take "vows of maiden purity" and he did not notice cloistered monks, who in their heads saw themselves as superior to others and held the whole world in contempt.

Monday, October 1

One has to go to the Novice Master to get letters that the gatekeeper brother receives from the mailman. Sometimes during the morning talk on asceticism the Father mentions the names of brothers who received correspondence. It turns out that this kind of public announcement embarrasses me greatly and I would prefer that my name not be announced too often. In our group oddities are sought out, evidence that somebody is a "changeling." Today fortunately I found out about a letter from my mother while passing the Novice Master in the corridor. As usual, the envelope had been cut open.

September 28

Dear Son,

Thank you for the letters. Although to tell the truth I get them only now and then, several at a time, after reading them I don't know which of them I should reply to. I am grateful to God for everything and also for having allowed me to fulfill the vow I had made when I was carrying you beneath my heart, when He accepted you to the monastery. You amaze me with some of your letters. I thought I knew you well, as your mother – the best of all your friends. Meanwhile what I am reading is pained. Your words do not have that warmth gushing from them, which there should be plenty of in your life.

I did not know that so many fears and anxieties could be lurking in so young a head. I personally believe that you are on the best path for happiness and salvation. No marriage, not even the happiest, can give you what the Convent gives. Jasna Góra is one of the most important spiritual oases in Poland, and you, in choosing the Order of St. Paul, can participate in the great work that is to be accomplished.

Be brave, that is the virtue I pray for on your behalf daily before the Miraculous Image of the Blessed Virgin Mary of Jasna Góra.

Your loving,
Mother

Wednesday, October 3

Sometimes, for no apparent reason, I feel anxiety. It can be caused by a look, by the plump, melancholy face of one of my companions. Among the gray plastered walls I begin to detect the presence of invisible forces, which so far I knew so little about. Now they stick to my skin like autumn dampness.

The Reverend Novice Master is adept in evoking these phantoms. He can, at his flaming conferences, bring up the appropriate dogma of the Catholic Church about the physical existence of the devil. When he speaks of hell every word breathes fire and smoke. After each such conference, our dreams are smeared with tar and sulfur.

It turns out that escape from the world into the monastery does not resolve anything yet. We can never get rid of the body, which is a source of temptation, the black temple of hidden wickedness. Demons in curved mirrors additionally multiply our specters. They make a ruckus, yell and dance in monk skulls. They behave like crazed monkeys in the Amazon delta. The devilish whisper knocks leaves off trees, and kindles a hurricane of vile temptations and misfortunes in our soul. As a novice, recently admitted to the mysteries of monastic life, I have to face these forces, hitting my head against the wall.

More than ever I feel the need every day to say the Litany to the Guardian Angels, to Michael the Archangel, who like Hercules, can take care of a flock of demons incarnating as cats, dogs and birds of prey. "*And he won't come back until they perish*" (Ps. 18, 38).

Friday, October 5

The Novice Master began today's conference with a sentence from St. Paul: "Now we see unclearly, as in a mirror, but later - face to face" (1 Cor 13, 12). He had in mind that our thoughts are not sufficiently clear when we try to understand the mysteries of faith. Our mind is unpredictable and capricious. The more we try to understand something, the more mind gets confused. To guard against the temptations of the devil, the body must obey our will. Hermits, including our patron Paul, accepted the thesis that the body is the enemy of the soul. Therefore, you need to overpower this enemy, bind it, to have control over it; impair it physically, so it would be in no condition to occupy the mind with its corporality.

A true anchorite should have no mercy for his body. St. Gregory of Nyssa felt that his body was "an inert and loathsome garment."

Saturday, October 7

It rained from early morning, I had the desire to write a letter to Krystyna. But the words escaped from beneath my pen, and those that suddenly floated up were inappropriate. It all ended with an attempt at a poem.

When it rains

As soon as it rains, the grace of angels drips
from the clouds,
you can hurry and collect them like small pearls.
Look how thickly grace showers from the heavens
onto the entire neighborhood,
just turn your umbrella upside down, and you'll gather
thousands for yourself and for those you love.
If you want to live with the angels, sometimes you have
to get wet,
when you hear it thunder, do not flee beneath a tree,
gather little pearls for yourself and for those you love.

Tuesday, October 9

Yesterday, while serving at table, I dropped a platter of kasha on the floor, in front of the prior's table. Everybody burst out laughing. The reader, who was reading aloud "The Glories of Mary" by St. Alphonsus Liguori thought that we were laughing at him. Scooping up the hot kasha with my bare hands back onto the dish, I thought that I should pick it up with my tongue like a dog, and eat it together with the dust straight off the floor. Terrified,

I wandered with the dish straight to the prior's table, instead of to the kitchen window. He cut me down quickly with a hand gesture, as though he were cutting nettles by the side of the path. My head was all awhirl. I stood in the middle of the refectory, like a pillar of salt, and mumbled something to myself senselessly. Fortunately, Brother Fabian, who hurrying over to the window, nudged me with his elbow, whispering, "Dummy, two more tables still have to be served."

Friday, October 12

Reading the biographies of saints, I conclude that there are more of them in the Catholic Church than there are fish in the Baltic Sea. I never heard of many of them. I will be able to get acquainted with many of them now. The half-hour, and sometimes more, of spiritual reading makes the saint-filled sky in my mind become ever more limitless. I had very poor contemplations on this point.

I associated saints with All Souls Day in November. With the lighting of candles on graves, with St. Anthony, the patron saint of lost things, with Midsummer night, when we jumped into the Warta River in June, to have the first summer swim. Meanwhile, Saints are flesh and blood people, who were able to resolve life's riddles in a relatively complete way.

Of the saints that I had read of thus far in Rev. Piotr Skarga, I am most impressed by the medieval saint Catherine of Siena (she lived from 1347 to 1380). She was a writer, diplomat and mystic in one person. She amazed popes and bishops, monks, merchants, craftsmen and peasants. She was the twenty-fourth child in the family of a Sienese dyer. Maybe that is why she was a woman without any hang-ups toward men. Her sense of her weakness and nothingness before God did not lead her to sorrow and complexes. Christ on the crucifix is her Lord, Master and Friend, and His pierced side; feet and hands are a book which teaches her love that is faithful and capable of sacrifice.

October 13

Dear Krystyna,

I'm not sure if I'm doing the right thing, turning to you with such a request. I still don't understand many things well, I try to clarify them by reading some books about the life of hermits, which I learned of from other books and from the lips of the spiritual guide himself I can't find in our library. I wish them so much that when it turns out that they are not available, I feel like a boxer in the ring, who gets a left hook to the jaw and is unable to hit back.

It finally occurred to me that I am in a religious order of hermits whose patron, Paul the First Hermit, is a saint who lived sixteen centuries ago. I asked our librarian for his biography, thinking that because he is "first", he will be overgrown with legends like a branch overgrown with flowers in the spring.

None of these things. Barely a small mention in the biography of St. Anthony, who had the opportunity to visit him shortly before he died in his hermitage. My request would be that I'd like to get at the books of hermits to have a better idea what motivated them to seek God alone. This is the twentieth century and I would like to carry some of their hermit sand in my shoes.

Saints Paul and Anthony lived in vile times, fled from a society that was falling apart. The world that surrounded them did not favor their interior needs. Our culture also promotes dissolution and secularization. So not much has changed since those times. Perhaps such a system of struggle between good and evil has always existed? Maybe the escape to the monastery is the only right choice? I would prefer to have more confidence in these contemplations. Perhaps I will find the seed of my salvation in the wisdom of those long-dead anchorites.

Your knowledge of church literature always impressed me. Maybe together we can reach the right source quicker. I am counting on your help very much.

Thank you for your beautiful letter, which uplifted my spirits.

With due respect,
Brother Modest

Tuesday, October 16

I ashamedly realized how great a role the senses play in my life. I touch my ears, neatly shaped shells and in the darkness of the night, I am delighted with the slightest murmur. From the small rhythmic breathing of my roommates I can infer the kind of dreams they are having. I react to the flight of a fly or a mosquito that wants to drink my blood. My ears also report to me about the Novice Master's quiet steps in the corridor, as he checks if the lights are out everywhere and if the whispers of conversations aren't wounding the monastic silence somewhere.

With my fingers I touch my cool forehead, elbows, knees, my warm abdomen. I stroke the wall by the bed with my hand; it is cold, hard, and silent. I want to nestle up to it with my whole body so that it will promise me before bedtime that it will stand watch by me all night. In the corridor the clock is already striking eleven. In the dark the brass tones of the clock spread very slowly. Before I fall asleep, I climb Jacob's ladder to the first cloud, rung by rung ... thirty-third, thirty-fourth, thirty-nine ...

Friday, October 19
It is probably the prompting of the devil or a tricky maneuver of my laziness, because thoughts are circling in my head that I don't have to make much effort to meet the demands made here. Imprisoned as if in a cage, I can't commit any act that would demean the dignity of another person. Other white mice would eat me that same evening.

For practical reasons, the Reverend Novice Master can't look inside my head, he would first have to saw it in half, then together with a specialist theologian he would urgently have to seek the cells contaminated by sin, those with a malicious pestilence raging in them.

I know it will never come to that. I do not exhibit any external signs by which the disease could be identified. Out of habit I walk in a file with others and do not stray to the sides. I say the rosary with the others. God is gracious; He won't throw us into hell for it.

Sunday, October 21

Mother's first visit. I could only see her for two hours after dinner. We were both very moved. My mother had wet cheeks. I felt a great attachment to her, but like a fool I kept my hands in my sleeves. To this moment I can't comprehend: if in reality we need each other, then why did she, systematically and persistently, try to persuade me to join the Order? Does she have some plans, ambitions, of which I know nothing?

No major changes at home. My younger brother now spends more time at home than on the sports field. Aunt Krystyna and Irena visit mother in the evenings, as always, and have a nice time together. On parting mom handed me two letters, which the monastery had sent back to the senders. One from Leszek K., addressed to Mr. Marcin Kowacz, the second from Zygmunt H. with a similar inscription on the envelope. I did not show mother my discontent, but my heart was painfully pricked. I hadn't started existing as a monk yet for the gatekeeper brother who was sending back correspondence, and as a civilian I wasn't yet a person worthy of his attention. I suppose that totally unaware of what had happened, he had passed a sentence on me.

Monday, October 22

The letters from my friends yesterday disturbed my sleep. Zygmunt H. and I have been pals for four years, basically since the sixth grade. Our schools, Number Thirteen and Eighteen, were in the same building. Day after day we met on the joint sports field. Zygmunt read a lot; I tried to match his pace. We exchanged books and opinions about Sienkiewicz, May, or Dickens. I felt guilty that I had not told him of my intention to go to the monastery. Zygmunt's cousin Lucyna looks more beautiful from year to year. She appears today in my mind as if alive, obsessively feminine.

Leszek and I became friends even earlier. Both of our mothers couldn't live without each other. They read everything that Rodziewiczówna and Conrad wrote. They went to the movies together and solved crossword puzzles together. Often Leszek and I wore the same striped shirts, leather suspenders, or Scout uniforms. Now I blushed with shame. I had broken the peer code of ethics, the youthful instinct to speak the truth.

Tuesday, October 24

I dreamed of my grandmother. The old lady was 89 years old when she went to the angels. I remember her cordially, because during the German occupation, my mother placed me in her care. The city often lacked food.

In Niewęgłowice, a small village near Wieluń, I lived with four uncles and aunt Leonora. I was a little tyke, running around and getting in their way; they did not always have time for me, or patience. But under grandma's watchful eye nothing bad ever happened to me. At first with her, then by myself, I took the geese out into the field and watched them, so they wouldn't nibble the green rye grain, or wander off into the neighbor's buckwheat or millet.

For many years, my grandmother was present at almost all the baby deliveries in the village. And together with her second husband, Janusz Klamer, she was present at all the funerals that went from the village to the cemetery. Today I dreamed of her, that she was as if worried about something, or maybe just lost in thought. She asked me to gather some nettles and strongly lash her back with them. She quickly took off, over her head, a gray, handmade wool sweater. A lot of weeds grew in the yard by the fence, but few nettles. I had to work at it a bit, to pluck them. I also wanted to explain to her that I am in a monastery now, and that Novice Master will be very unhappy that she is exposing herself. Her body was smooth and pale as alabaster. She replied that the reason she came to me, is because she is still in Purgatory and asks that I pray for her.

I was very scared upon waking. I really liked Grandma, but that period when I lived with her was sad for me. I longed for my mother, who visited me once or twice a year; I missed my younger brother and my father. Instead of growing up among my peers I was growing up among adults. My uncles often disappeared, probably went to the guerrillas, and I stayed alone on the farm. I was afraid of the empty attic, of the barn with its rampaging mice, of the cows tugging at the chains attached by iron rings to the beams, of the horses neighing at night and the squealing pigs. I had to behave like an adult, though I was only a seven-year-old boy.

Saturday, October 28

I get a lot of benefits from my spiritual readings. Books about saints are easy, similar patterns repeat in each one- the wind of virtues always blows from the valleys of darkness toward the rocky peaks bathed in the rays of the sun. Books about martyrs are more colorful. Typically, one dramatic moment in the life of the martyr decides the future eternal glory of the saint. Martyrs do not have to perform miracles, their death and love of God is sufficient evidence that they are already in heaven.

In the case of maiden martyrs the scenario is arranged a little differently. Almost all do not succumb to the wicked proposals of tyrants, they prefer to walk barefoot on burning coals and be ripped apart by wild animals than to lose their sacred virginity. Some manage to have a vision of the parting heavens already at the moment of death and watch the angels floating down from on high to greet them.

Devotees have a harder time. They work very hard all their lives, establish hermitages in remote places, monasteries on the outskirts of cities, orphanages for abandoned infants or girls who have lost their virtue. Still others establish schools and universities, passing the torch of Christian doctrine from generation to generation. Becoming a holy devotee in the Universal Church is not easy. After a death caused by prolonged illness, old age or anemia, they still have to get famous through their miracles. Document books thick as the Napoleonic Code, hearings in the Roman Curia, and the endless requests and prayers of the faithful for their beatification finally bear fruit in their elevation to the altars.

October 29

Dear Aunt Celina,

I am a bit sad after reading your letter. Something must have changed very dramatically, which I don't grasp. I remember a different picture of you. Over the past three years, when we were to go to Niegów- Samaria with Janek, we were filled with joy. We knew that time spent with you as the gardener would be nice and interesting. In the large garden that you tended, there were always so many interesting shrubs and fruit trees, vegetables and greens, that there was no way to be able to taste them all. Walking with rakes to pull up weeds, we stuffed ourselves with gooseberries or raspberries, sweet cherries and apricots. We climbed up the spreading apple trees to shake the branches and gather the fallen apples into baskets.

Even when weeding the vegetable beds we weren't bored. You could eat a raw cucumber or a warm, sun-drenched tomato or crunchy radish. After a holiday spent with you we returned sun-tanned and relaxed, better fed than at home. From time to time we would get a thrashing from you, but only when the devil got in under our skin. I remember how once in a big wind your veil flew off your head. I do not know why that really got you upset. I then saw a few black and gray strands on your head.

But there was also fun. We went with sister Ruta and Mrs. Janina, called "protruding ears" by us, to the forest to pick mushrooms. They took us along for assistance. Janina, though supposedly absent-minded, found the most mushrooms. I gathered berries and carried the basket with the Boletus mushrooms. Janek circled around sister Ruta like a bumblebee, constantly asking: "Sis, is this a Boletus Luteus or a Boletus mushroom?"

And she: "neither the one nor the other, just a toadstool . . . just a yellow Blewit ... just an edible Morel ... just a puffball. " Thanks to her I can still recite by heart the names of a dozen mushrooms, that I didn't have the foggiest idea what they looked like.

In your letter you treated me like a mosquito that had been closed up inside a church after sunset. You are already in the Congregation of the Samaritan Sisters more than twenty years, and I only a few months, but that does not mean that my decision required less sacrifice. And secondly, I learned already what the difference is between a Congregation and an Order. An Order is like a higher form of commitment to God, it requires total concentration, contemplation, in other words maximum mental effort.

In Congregations the work is manual or administrative, as for instance in education. One spends more time with people every day, thus eliminating the monotony of monastic life. Care for the sick and handicapped also gives satisfaction and contentment because it is visible to others. Self-Improvement in a contemplative Order is not spectacular, requires more patience and self-denial. Climbing up the ladders of virtue and self-mortification can't be expressed in statistics.

The confessor and the preacher help those who have a handicapped soul, those who have eyes but cannot see, who have good hearing, but are deaf to the mercy of the Holy Spirit. And you didn't take this difference into consideration. Maybe I should not express myself on these topics, I'm in the Order too short a time, but I am trying to defend the environment in which I now find myself, and our Order's patron saint, the First Hermit, although he lived in the sixth century.

Please greet sister Florencja cordially and ask her to write to me.

May God and all the saints be with you,
Brother Modest

October 19

Dear Modest - Marcin,

I am sorry that I can't help you much in expanding your reading list on the subject of hermits. The information which I still have in my head comes from courses on the writings of the Fathers of the Church, which I attended for two semesters. The lecturer at that time was prof. Ignacy Toruń, a Jesuit, very well liked by students. On the occasion of discussing various topics important materials would appear, such as "Gerontikon, or the Book of Old People", also "The Life of Saint Anthony" written by Athanasius of Alexandria. The professor highly valued the work of John Cassian titled "Twenty Four Conversations" and "Letters of St. Jerome " in the study by Rev. J.Czuj. I recall the work on early Christian monasticism by prof. F. Bogdan, "The Genesis and development of the monastic cloister." I doubt, however, whether these works can be found in your novitiate library, which focuses mainly on hagiographic and devotional literature.

I sincerely congratulate you on approaching your interests ambitiously from the start. The thirst for knowledge hasn't damaged anybody's liver or heart yet. I see your Mother often. Recently Sister Justyna, a Samaritan Nun, your likeable Aunt, was with your mother for two days. She asked anxiously about you, and we in turn asked about Sister Florencja, who began her novitiate seven months ago. So you're not alone on the path leading to the discovery of the truth about yourself, God and the world.

Give it some thought, maybe you could write your cousin a letter. When she lived in the apartment with you and your family on St. Anne's Street, you were like brother and sister. Now it's time to assist her in similar hardships, which you yourself have undertaken. You should not feel isolated in this noble journey.

As always, with sincere devotion,
Krystyna

As he handed me the letter the Reverend Novice Master looked slightly subdued. I guess he was not comfortable with my asking people outside the monastery for information. But he could not condemn my natural hunger for knowledge.

Wednesday, October 31

I am spooked by the thought that even here, in this quiet retreat saturated with prayer, carnal lust does not expire within me. The ascetic ideals of the Novice Master and his exhortation to purity resurrect prohibited memories rather than suppress them. In my mind's eye I see the faces of women I would like to embrace, kiss on the mouth, cuddle up to their breasts and hips.

I remember what my father once told an older colleague of his on the eve of retirement: - "Władek, as long as you have the desire to love young ladies, so long you know you're alive. Every woman feels through her skin that she can rely on you." I do not want that saying to ever refer to me.

Thursday, November 1

At dinner I choked. Probably a piece of cooked tomato skin stuck in my esophagus. I was coughing it up all evening long. I was ashamed that I was turning attention on myself. I drank water and swallowed pieces of dry bread to remove the obstruction from my throat. Nothing helped. After the last prayers, I quickly ran to my cell, so I would already be in bed by the time the others had arrived. At night, the cough woke me up from time to time.

I realized how much I depended on the people I was with. Three months ago I never dreamed that they could help me with anything, or harm me. Today I could read the mocking expression on their faces: this starveling ate too greedily, and the Angel of Justice meted out an appropriate punishment to him.

Friday, November 2

The tomato peel slid into my stomach together with some saliva. Tonight, after the lights are off, I will rebuke my entire body with a real leather whip, let it writhe in pain. Let it not expose me to ridicule any more. After all I am here to take care of my soul, not its outer shell, which the bugs will eat in the grave anyhow. In the dark my body has no contours, is barely visible, perhaps it's even unreal. I will find out about that when I slice it with my whip. Throughout the centuries our monks repeated, during their Friday flagellations: remember, you're a man and you will die. *Memento mori.*

Yesterday I received a letter from Janusz P., a close friend with whom I used to do my homework, went to the movies, and his mother often invited me to dinner.

October 24

Dear Marcin,

Only a few sentences in a hurry. My piano teacher will be here in a minute. As usual, I didn't practice everything she as-

signed me. I told you many times that I did not really feel like practicing with her. There's a slight old maid whiff to her. Mom does not understand that. It's her distant cousin and mom wants to support her financially.

But this is not the reason for this letter. November eleventh is St. Marcin's Day - your name day. I want to wish you all the best on your new path. I miss you. It was easier to do our homework together and the time flew by faster. Greetings from your friends at the Jasna Góra Altar Boy Circle. They are proud that you were admitted to the novitiate. Anyway, you're not the first. Two years ago Father Honoratus succeeded in placing both of the Tyramiński brothers. One of them plays the organ quite well. No doubt you'll bump into each other in the monastery.

Keep well,

Janusz P.

P. S.
Marcin, please, write me what your daily life looks like. I'm curious.

Saturday, November 3
I did not drag my feet in getting out a reply. Just yesterday evening I described to Janusz the beautiful illusion I live in.

Dear Janusz ,

It was a great pleasure to get your letter and name day wishes. By the way, I should mention that in the spirit of the novice tradition the name Marcin has ceased to exist for me. On the day of my enrobing (Your mother was a witness) I received a new name - Modest. In the liturgical calendar St. Modest doesn't come around until June 15. He was the teacher of a young boy and martyr, Saint Wit. And in general, "modestus" in Latin means the same as modest, shy, not elevating oneself above others. I have come to like that name, because it very accurately describes who I should be now.

In your letter you ask me to write about the way of life here. The worst thing for me is getting up at five o'clock in the morning. Then there is a half-hour of meditation, reading the breviary in Latin, which I still am unable to read well, nor understand. Immediately afterward the Mass begins. And Holy Communion, with a half-hour of thanksgiving. Breakfast is at eight, at nine the recitation of the Litany to the Guardian Angels. You are probably surprised why the litany to the spirits is right before noon, with whom no one meets nor asks for anything.

According to what the Novice Master says, for sure they are not "a nebulous vapor, or nothingness." They are stronger in spirit than people, they have no need for food or reproduction, and they do not to sink into depression and are free from death. It is worthwhile to make friends with them, they are obliging and never betray. Believe me, these astral spirits are all around and are as plentiful as butterflies in May over a poppy field, you just have to sharpen your sight to see them.

In the morning we also have a conference, in other words a lecture about the ascetic life. As you can surmise, almost every day I look into the dictionary to find out what all these new words, that I am learning, mean. At ten we have the Way of the Cross (six times a week, the exception is Sunday). At a quarter to twelve a self-examination of conscience, very detailed, about the small dust particles of transgressions that have happened to us throughout the day.

At noon we recite the breviary that is the Sext and None, in the choir while standing. Then dinner, when you can eat as much as you want of noodles with cabbage, or potatoes with bacon and sour milk. After lunch there's recreation, i.e. a stroll around the garden if the weather is nice, or conversation in the large hall, where suddenly everyone wants to talk with everybody about everything. At two thirty a spiritual reading, usually biographies of saints, on which it is best to model one's life. At three Vespers in Latin, consisting of five psalms, an antiphon, hymn and the Magnificat. At four thirty another Conference with the Novice Master about the Constitution or the history of the Pauline Order.

At six another meditation, supper and a visit to the Blessed Sacrament. Then recreation, which always seems too short, even though it lasts an hour. At eight the Matutinum, that is, the main part of the breviary: 9 psalms with antiphons and nine readings, and the Te Deum. Although for the true monk prayer never hangs heavy, it is a real marathon. For nearly an hour or longer we have to articulate out loud the Latin vowels and consonants, and blend them into not very rhythmic verses. Fifteen minutes after nine the bell rings for strict silence (Silen-

tium strictissimum). You can then communicate only by writing, or a gesture, not even by a whisper.

If you're not exhausted yet by this relatively long order of the day, you're better than me. I often checked the rules and wait for the bell, for the knock on the door and I hurry to make it on time down the long corridors to chapel, the conference room or the refectory. I think that over time I will acquire the routine of a true monk and my day will flow smoothly and freely. I will not have to look at the cheat sheet pinned to my sleeve.

Please give my cordial regards to your parents and brother Ryszard,

Marcin,
Or if you prefer, brother Modest

Wednesday, November 7

I still can't understand the great fascination that the Novice Master has for the life of the little St. Therese of Lisieux, the Carmelite nun. As is usual in the biographies that I have read so far, she was the youngest of nine children. Sickly, she needed a rural wet nurse, who could strengthen her body. Her father was a watchmaker, and her mother was a lace maker. The saint left behind a journal, the "Story of a Soul", which everyone here is reading with great interest. I joined the line for the book. I wonder how I will react to it, although in this male monastic order I would prefer to model myself on personalities of my sex.

During her last visit, my mother reminded me of

the obligation to write a letter to Father Albert. I was under his care for nearly two weeks, at the Pauline Fathers monastery in Ohpohroof. My mother met him by chance in the sacristy and he probably asked about me.

November 7

Dear Father Albert,

I wonder how it happened that three months have passed, and I still haven't written to you. Those weeks spent in Ohpohroof, under your care, were the best way for me to get acquainted with monastic life. I did not participate fully in the daily schedule, but I could see what was happening from hour to hour. I spent more time in church and in the convent chapel. Serving at mass I heard at least half a dozen sermons addressed to the parishioners. I liked the walks together with you down to the river and lake overgrown with rushes and Sweet Flag. You taught me to play chess and checkers. I asked you dozens of questions about religion and the Order. Now I see how useful those discussions were. One piece of your advice in particular stuck in my mind: "If you don't know something, take a book and read."

Thus far, "spiritual reading" is one of the points in the novice program that does not bore me. In second place I would put meditation, because I can indulge my imagination. I am also slowly improving in the recitation of the breviary in Latin and in the readings during the evening Matutinum, which are as long as Moses' beard. It just bothers me that my lips utter words, whose meaning I do not yet comprehend. I'm delighted, on the other hand, with the Latin rhythm of the sentences, which is seductive with its ancient distinctness.

I still have problems getting up early in the morning. My mother always had a hard time getting me up in the morning for school. Now I am praying to the Virgin Mary that the superiors transfer you to Lehshnyoof. In my spare time I'd make a beeline to your cell for a small game of chess. After all, I have already beaten you two or three times. Our Spiritual Guide does not like us to write or receive letters from others. But I think a letter from a Pauline and a priest should not cause me harm.

I cordially greet you and wait for your letters, which will be filled with titles of books recommended by you, Father, for me to read.

Brother Modest

Saturday, November 10

The letter from Mrs. Irena came by mail, the Novice Master opened and read it. When he handed me the envelope he expressed concern about my overly voluminous correspondence. He would prefer that it were less.

November 5

Dear Modest,

I delayed nearly two months with my reply to your letter. I came to the conclusion that even more than my womanish advice you need focus, inner silence. The Novice Master can give you all the necessary advice that you might need in the initial period. You don't have to worry about St. Teresa of Avila too much now. Her discourse on the mystical life, given the stage at which you are at this moment, will only serve to discourage you. The logic of the people of that time was quite different from ours. To understand this will take you some time.

I recommend, however, that instead of reading the works of St. Teresa of Jesus who was a doctor of the Universal Church, you get acquainted with the "diaries" of God's Servant S.M. Faustina. She only had a basic education, but she was able to explain the qualities of Divine Mercy and the simple, very ordinary economy of our salvation better than the theologians could.

You have nine months left to think about what you want to do with your life. You entered the path of self-improvement, and that choice is never easy. You first have to rid your interior like a neglected garden, of weeds, prickly thistles and dried stalks. And in their place plant healthy seed.

Take advantage of the opportunities being offered to you in the novitiate. Now you do not have to worry about your food, a roof over your head, school. It's the most beautiful time of your life. Do try, day by day, to be more honest toward yourself and others, more just and loyal to the Order. Deepen your faith, hope and love; without these virtues, our interior is dry and barren.

Your letter made me realize one more thing: our conversations with your mom did not just flow like moisture down the walls, but it oozed into your ears. We are therefore the co-mothers of your vocation, the co-seducers of your dreams. From a distance *we can only help you in that we will be minimally present in your mind and your isolation. In the monastery they symbolically cut your hair off so you can begin to think independently, so that, alone with yourself, like a cactus in the desert, you can withstand all the changes in temperature and the inconveniences of everyday life.*

You have to persevere, be with yourself to the end.

This is your nagging aunt's wish for you,
Irena

Irena's letter came at a very good time, but I couldn't get myself together after reading it. It seemed that everybody was working on my improvement, as if I were a competitor on an important team. The dietician tells me what I need to eat, to mortify my body effectively, the coach says how many times I have to circle around the stadium, to be in shape, the team captain instructs me how to center the ball in front of the opponent's goal. Except that what I am doing, is still not what I should be doing. The Novice Master is not happy that I get a lot of correspondence. Mother complains that I don't write enough, and I am tossing about like a mouse in a cage and still do not see the path that leads to the heights of perfection. All the saints whom I have been reading about are from another world, and imitating them in the monastery would make me a freak.

I cannot walk barefoot in the snow, as St. Wenceslaus used to, because socks and shoes are part of the monk's outfit. I can't sit in a basket and not wash myself, as Simeon Stylites did, because they'd throw a stinker like that out of the Order in a week.

In the novitiate, you can only go to hell because you wanted to please a woman, or you broke a coffee jug and thus violated the vow of poverty, or you didn't obey the Prior, when he ordered you to jump from the belfry down to the courtyard in front of the church. A monk's unbridled pride is best tamed by a dunking in an ice hole.

Sunday, November 11
In the liturgical calendar, the feast of Marcin, the prince on a white horse, is my name day. I dream of a hot bath, an enamel bathtub filled to the brim with fragrant soapy foam, and a rough sponge, with which I could scrub my knees that are as hard as a horse's hoof. I think that the angels don't admit stinking, sweaty bums from the street to Paradise. My idea of purgatory is associated with a huge lake filled with various disinfectants, and every sweaty body has to swim across it to get to the wide beach leading to heaven. Clothes will no longer be needed, because we won't be ashamed. Shame is initiated by original sin. Adam and Eve defiled our innocence. I fled to the monastery because I'm ashamed of naked women. All my colleagues, who have overcome the barrier of shame, are unable to stand it in the monastery for more than one day.

Holy Virgin of virgins, pray for us.

Monday, November 12

Yesterday was my birthday. I completed the sixteenth year of my life, so starting today I am trampling on the heels of number seventeen. Everybody wants me to be grown up already, be a man, they keep gluing wings on me, they want me to fly and shoo away hail clouds.

They say that Mozart, when he was 11 years old, played harpsichord duets with his sister. He was seven years old when he composed his first piece – the Minuet and Trio. Chopin, before he turned 16, amazed Warsaw's elite with his unusual way of playing the piano, and began to compose his first sonatas.

I think it is my aunt who finds these comparisons to her taste. It has probably not occurred to her that in my case this is pure irony of fate. Already at the first audition when voices were being selected for the novitiate chorus it came to light that I do not have a good ear that an elephant stepped on my ear. And just because I like to read and write a diary, it does not follow that I will be a poet or a novelist.

Wednesday November 14

Sometimes, when nothing interesting happens in our lives, we turn to memories. You can always find something that you did not want to think about before.

Yesterday before I fell asleep, my head was filled with the first weeks after the passage of the Russian troops and the chasing out of the Nazis. In the countryside, where my mother sent me during the war, they started organizing a school. There was only one teacher in the whole village. The school was organized in mid-March. At first we all attended one class (about 30 children), then two, when we were divided into two age groups.

We learned the alphabet, forming letters into words, and words into short sentences. Four copies of Falski's Primer were our textbooks. The same teacher taught Polish and the multiplication table. After three and a half months of that training I got admitted to fourth grade.

When toward the end of May my mother brought me to Częstochowa, I was admitted to the same class. For two days I sat like a dumb bunny in the third row, but when the teacher told me to read the reader aloud, the drama began. I tried to spell the words out, and groaned with every syllable. The class burst out laughing. The teacher called my mother in and demanded that I immediately take a tutor or she wouldn't advance me to the next grade.

Since then, I'm constantly under the impression that whenever I start something new, I'm already late and I need to catch up as soon as possible. That is why I hate it when somebody tries to hurry me up.

Thursday, November 15
Thursdays are beautiful, because we go for long walks in the vicinity. Today, after an all night snowfall, the

fields were white. They resembled a soft, fluffy carpet that was spread as wide as the eye could see. A carpet that only monks dare tread, dressed in white robes and black cloaks. A frosty wind pinched our cheeks.

Instead of the Novice Master his assistant, Father Antoni Soból, was with us. Shorter than the Novice Master by a head, with slower movements and pronunciation, he gave the impression of a discountenanced cleric, who had no use for this role of guardian of such a swarm of monastery greenhorns. In moments when he did not control himself, he could be annoying and sarcastic toward those around him.

Our route never changed much. Today, however, because of the frozen ground, we took short cuts and got to the place in an hour. It was open terrain, we could loiter over the fields, some looked for a boulder or a felled tree, to sit down and relax.

The thick, heavy coats, which pressed heavily against our arms during the march, now protected us from the cold. It was an opportunity to get to know our new substitute guardian better. The conversation was going nowhere; our new guardian angel had no ready anecdotes or stories up his sleeve. I tried to remember some fragments of conversations between my mother, aunt Krystyna and Mrs. Irena. They mystified, fantasized galore every evening.

So I asked Father Antoni:

- What is the Mystical Body of the Church?

For a moment he was silent, hesitated – that was my impression in any case. Then, smiling tolerantly, he said:

- You have to wait a bit for the complete answer, brother. Those kinds of definitions are explained in the class on dogmatics during the first or second year of theology. In the novitiate the main thing is to understand Pauline spirituality and the implementation of the monastic life. It is best to recite the breviary and rosary, read the biographies of saints, and imitates them.

After me Brother Fabian jumped out with a similar question.

- And was St. Thomas a philosopher or a theologian?

The response was very similar:

- First you have to get your high school diplomas, learn Latin, Polish and mathematics.

- What do we need math for?

- You need a bit of math to help you use the abacus.

- And what do we need the abacus for? The questioner insisted.

- When, brother Fabian, they make you the treasurer in the monastery, you will have to count and pay, subtract, save and calculate how much of everything you need per person.

In the end Father Assistant let himself be caught up in the discussions. The fresh, frosty air makes the brain work more efficiently. It is also easier to get to the crux of the problem with a question. We had fun looking at the ruddy cheeks of our new instructor, who really wanted to do the right thing and to shine as a good example.

We returned in small, scattered groups saying our rosary as usual. Father Antoni Soból walked with the first group, holding in his right, frozen hand the beads of his wooden rosary.

Saturday, November 17

My parents' life consisted of hard work and endless worries. Father worked hard from dawn to dusk, walked up and down a fifteen foot wooden ladder, tearing the tendons in his legs to smear heavy white-wash on the ceilings in factories or churches, and Mother kept wracking her brains how to make ends meet from one pay day to the next. She knitted sweaters, hats and warm socks for us.

So what right have I here, with a food-stuffed belly, separated from the world by a monastery wall, to dare to complain about anything else? Had fate not taught me the hard rules of existence in the years that have passed? How is it then that dreams, strange specters and distortions are now appearing in my head? The more I say the rosary, repeat the litanies, walk on my knees from one Station of the Cross to the next, the more unruly associations and impurities awaken within me. Is this what the dark path leading to perfection is all about, that the Great Teresa of Carmel wrote about? If the delights of one's own body stand in the way, I should scold them with discipline, enslave them with fasting, so that the devils won't lead me into temptation any more.

Jesus, lashed so many times by His executioners, have mercy on us.

Wednesday, November 21

Through the window I see three freezing sparrows on the roof. They snuggle up to each other and hide their tiny heads under their wings. My thoughts again fly home. I try to drown out the inner restlessness that circles around me like a fly, and has no desire to buzz off. I started to write a letter to my mother.

November 21

Dear Mom,

What worries me is that you hardly write me. I miss you all a lot. Inside the monastery walls one can go crazy without any thoughts of you. I am concerned that from time to time domestic strife may occur between you. I do not like those tensions between you. I am helpless at this distance, and I would not be able to live a single hour here, knowing that anyone of you might get hurt. Father loves you very much, you must be patient with him.

My dear Mother, the shoes you spent so much money on are already falling apart. After the last two strolls and the rainy weather they softened up entirely, and the paper is coming out of them. My heart skipped a beat when I saw the heel coming off. I became very attached to these shoes. I thought that I would be able to walk in them for at least two years.

I was extremely happy with the news that Father got a job at the railway station. Steady work and pay will certainly help you to maintain financial stability. Now you don't have to rely on casual labor and suck up to capricious customers.

Hugs and kisses
Your son

P.S. Mom, do not forget to insert a few postage stamps in your letter. Those that you left me are just about gone.

Saturday, November 24

Our spiritual father, like a single mystical cloud, sprinkles us with the snow of his instructions, good advice, and lofty recommendations. Sometimes he scares us with hell; it often reminds me of the jungle painted by Henri Rousseau, a French painter. Rousseau in his entire life had never been in a real jungle, he painted it from his imagination, based on the plants he saw in a botanical garden.

The Novice Master also has not been to the hell that he describes to us, that is why his devil is often funny, instead of scary. His hell fire is afraid of real flames, his tar is not black, and his devils bug their eyes out, as if they didn't know how to properly torture the souls of the damned.

With the persistence worthy of a Girolamo Savonarola our spiritual guide would like to bring us to the altar with quick steps, where, prostrating on the floor, we would reject the right to own any property, the right to fall in love with a woman and solemnly swear to blind obedience. Thin and wiry like a March deer, his neck stretched out toward the stars, he inflames our meager ambitions, pulls our ears as if we were a herd of unruly goats. But his whip, twisted of pious words, does not wound our skin; it dissolves like his warm breath on the wind.

I think that if he somewhat slowed the pace of his conference monologues, and instead of lowering his eyelids looked straight into our eyes, he would notice that there is only as much strength in us, as there is sense in our heads.

Human habits and tendencies cannot be eradicated from the soul in a week. Rather, they should be plucked one leaf at a time, until the root withers. Substances, over which we have little control percolate in our bodies, excite our senses, warm the imagination, which we haven't yet learned to control.

Virtue requires a clear definition of what good and evil are, if our thoughts are not organized, evil spreads in them like crab grass.

Tuesday, November 27

For several days, as if by the touch of a magic wand, I've been in a cheerful mood. Without any rational reason, I felt like creating mischief. In conversations with colleagues I try to make them laugh. As almost everyone here is hypersensitive and easily offended - I try to dramatize the normal things so we can laugh at them. However, the faces of my companions are made of rubber of the kind tires are produced, rubber that is not too flexible. In order not to offend anyone, I make jokes about myself.

Yesterday when the lights went out, I played a popular tune on my teeth in the pin-drop silence:

A kid from Cracow had horses seven,
He went to war, and was left with one.

At first my roommates, already covered with their blankets, did not know what was happening. The bed springs started squeaking, so they must have been listening. In the dark the drumming on my teeth sounded light and resonant.

I learned to play on my teeth quite by accident. I first observed it when one of the boys in an institution for the retarded operated by the Samaritan Sisters in Niegów near Warsaw, tapped out lively tunes. He could play with both hands. He had a very large skull, strongly protruding jaws and large teeth like a bear. He was great at it, a real virtuoso. I tried imitating him for many months. But my tappings were lifeless, with no melody. Until one day, by chance, I figured out how to combine melody with the rhythm I was tapping. Since then, I entertain myself with this amusing art for art's sake.

Wednesday, November 28

Today I read an awfully cute story in "The Lives of the Saints" by the Rev. Piotr Skarga, about a holy Black man, who was a wrestler and leader of a gang of thieves. Admonished in a dream by his guardian angel he joined a monastery. One day, four bandits came and began robbing the monastery starting with St. Moses' cell – that was the name given to him in the monastery. The former gang leader took care of them splendidly. He tied them up with ropes and went to ask his father Prior, what to do with them. They were from the same gang that he had once led. Repentant because their transgression was forgiven, the robbers converted and asked for admission to the monastery.

In "The Spiritual Food" however, the author refers to the great temptations of the flesh, with which the devils molested the holy giant and concludes that "filthy dreams, when there is no authorization for them, nor any loving in them, are no sin" and "the Lord God ... permits such temptations for our humility." I was delighted with that statement, because already several times in my dreams there was a similar Merry-Go-Round with all sorts of unsightliness.

Friday, November 30

Brother Salvatore finally gave me the "Story of a Soul" by Saint Theresa of the Child Jesus. He kept the book for over a month. When asked what he thought about it, he snapped "those are readings for Postulants in a female convent, not for monks." Nonetheless the diary of "the holy tiny Carmelite" from the very first pages fascinated me.

Born in Normandy, she lost her mother very early. Her older sister Pauline raised her. Not for long, however, because when the whole family moved to Lisieux, and established contacts with the Carmelite nuns, Pauline decided to join that Order. Soon, the 15 years and three months old Theresa joined her. Their third sister, Maria Marcin (Sister Maria of the Sacred Heart) was already in the monastery.

The departure of the youngest daughter from her ailing father, and because she was a minor (an amazing fact in our times), she needed the approval of the bishop. Theresa was admitted to Carmel April 9, 1888, during Easter, on the liturgical feast of the Annunciation. According to the design of Providence the saint was to be alive only ten years behind the convent walls in Lisieux. "The Story of a

Soul" made an impression on me because it is very close to our times, and not so general as the two and three page biographies in the lives of Rev. Skarga. It reflects the interior of the saint making difficult decisions from day to day. It also emboldened me to continue my own notes and to be honest and direct in them.

Sunday, December 2

It snowed all night. In the garden the branches bent under the weight of the snow. Wherever the eye stretched it was white, like the paintings of Fałat. The earth was covered with the white veil of innocence. Here and there lazy, gray chimney smoke. I was bursting with joy from inside. I wanted to wade knee-deep in the snow. In my white robe, with the white hood on my head, no one would notice me jumping over the monastery fence, the neighbor's fence, and the road piled high with snow drifts. As if it were a mad race through the woods I would bruise my knees and elbows on the pine trees.

Today, during the feast of the Virgin Mary of Candlemas, I would probably meet her in an open glade, amidst a pack of wolves heating their frosted noses by the light of her candle.

The bell sounded in the corridor, it is already five minutes to three, time for vespers. I can hear the doors open and close, as the brothers emerge from their cells and head to the chapel.

During the recitation of Psalm 126 we took a break at the verse marked with an asterisk. The right side started, the left continued. After some time the single, out of rhythm voices merged and evened out. The Psalm is a prayer for the return from Babylonian captivity to the land of the fathers; it is also the prayer of the internally oppressed.

When the Lord brought back the captives to Zion, *
  we were like men who dreamed
Our mouths were filled with laughter,
  * Our tongues with songs of joy.
Then it was said among the nations: *
"The Lord has done great things for them."
The Lord has done great things for us *
and we are filled with joy.

Restore our fortunes, O Lord, *
Like streams in the Negev.
Those who sow in tears, *
will reap with songs of joy.
He who goes out weeping,
carrying seed to sow,*
Will return with songs of joy,
carrying sheaves with him.

Tuesday, December 4

In the Book of Psalms of the Old Testament I read a few texts, which we often recite during the breviary hours. The translations of Rev. Wujek appeared almost simultaneously with "The Lives of the Saints," of Rev. Piotr Skarga. The old Polish of this period is beautiful. I am angry with myself for reciting these verses in Latin, not always comprehending their deep meaning.

Were it not for this blind obedience, which I will soon hang around my neck like a dog collar, I would revolt and demand that Leopold Staff's newest translation be used for the recitation of the breviary. Then for sure I would stop swinging about the ceiling with my fluttering thoughts, and I would carefully follow every word of King David, the greatest poet in the Old Testament.

For sure I will now look more often in the Latin dictionary to understand words that occur frequently. Two years of Latin in Henryk Sienkiewicz High School is not much, but I'm already familiar with the language and now I can adjust to the pronunciation. The Latin of the psalms and fragmentary reading from the fathers of the Church is different from what we learned in high school, using excerpts from Ovid and Cicero.

Thursday, December 6
During the afternoon conference, and lecture on the history of the Order, the Reverend Novice Master returned again to the biography of Saint Paul the First Hermit. He holds the patron of the Order up as a model.

Each Order has its own distinguishing characteristics, their own motivation to act. We are an eremitic order, cloistered, formed in accordance with the provisions of canon law and additional provisions in the constitution. Our fathers also accepted one of the oldest rules in the Church, the Rule of St. Augustine, as the basis of our existence.

The Paulines belong to the great family of contemplative orders, which include the Cistercians, Trappists and Camaldolites. None of these Orders gets involved in missionary work.

During the conference, I asked the Novice Master the following question:

"How is it that, in contrast to the three monastic families, which build their monasteries in remote places, the Paulines choose big cities, arrange indulgences and find themselves in the center of religious activity? At Jasna Góra they are the confessional and pulpit for all of Poland.

Our spiritual guide explained that this is happening in the spirit of the Order. The Paulines as hermits do not go outside the monastery; it is the people who visit them in the churches, seeking spiritual consolation and forgiveness of sins. St. Paul behaved in a similar manner. He agreed to a visit by St. Anthony, but did not go with him to other hermitages.

Thanks to that visit St. Anthony told the world about the good deeds of that man of God, who for almost a hundred years stayed in the desert which was unfriendly to man and beast.

Friday, December 7

I want to find out how my body will behave during a strict fast. For breakfast I drink black coffee without sugar. For lunch I eat a half bowl of soup and fish without vegetables and potatoes. For dinner I settled for sour milk. It is Friday, and I should also follow the injunction for strict silence.

It was not until late in the evening that I felt the frog of hunger throw its weight around in my stomach. I silenced it with tap water. During the evening I had the satisfaction of conscience that my Friday was like Good Friday, when the Mother of Sorrows assisted Jesus in his sufferings. Nor did I spare my own skin, when, after the lights were turned off, the body had to be whip-lashed.

Saturday, December 8

I'm trying again, at table, to repeat yesterday's experiment, giving up half of the dishes served. After entering the novitiate, my waist expanded and my cheeks rounded out. The change that occurred in my life reflected in my appearance. From a very active life at school and on the sports field I suddenly changed over to a lifestyle of low physical activity. I began to increasingly look like a pig that the farmer is preparing to sell. Every wolf can be thrown on its knees through hunger. I have to do the same with myself.

Let my body not tense up so much. The same rigor applies to it that I subject my soul to. Greater moderation in meeting physical needs and a redoubled effort when it comes to prayer, concentration and internal commitment to the activities prescribed by the rule of the given day. Through fasting the saints prepared their bodies for true asceticism, and closer contact with the angels. Like storks, from the valley of mediocrity, they raised their sluggishness to the heights of perfection.

Three years ago neighbors raised a ruckus that a statue was weeping in the church of the Pauline fathers in the Chapel of the Sacred Heart. Breathlessly I ran into the church, and found a crowd of kneeling and praying women. I pressed my forehead against the bars and stared intensely at the melancholy face of Jesus. After a few minutes I was sure that a stream of tears was flowing down the divine cheek. I was even worried that it might wash away the paint on the figure. Pleased, I ran to tell my mother about this incident. Mama repeated this with great emotion to my aunt and Mrs. Krystyna. That night I fell asleep exhilarated. I thought that I had been singularly honored. No doubt I dreamed of a cherub's face red as fire.

Monday, December 11
I gathered a bit of energy to write a letter to my cousin, of the Samaritan Order of nuns. Mother and her friends were preparing us to go into Holy Orders. Although we lived together, my mother took steps to ensure that we were never left alone. Jadwiga was older than me by a year, she learned knitting, and she had a lot of girlish charm. I liked her a little, but I dared not

tell her that. In the novitiate she was given the name Florencja.

Dear Sister Florencja,

You often appear in my thoughts. Seven months have passed since our parting. Before going to the novitiate, I really wanted to meet you. I wanted to know how you are coping in the congregation? How is collective life affecting your mental health and well being? I don't know if you remember that we promised to exchange letters and to help each other on the new path? I can see based on my own experience that the novitiate as a probation period demands a lot of self-denial, and the dislodging of contradictions from one's life. In preparing for the monastic life one cannot be vain, stubborn, inconsistent and scatterbrained like a clown in a circus, conceited among those who are learning to be humble, tactlessly talkative with those who do not over use words and love silence. In my own way, as I assimilate the new rules, I try to grapple with all these difficulties.

From Aunt Justyna's letter I learned that your novitiate lasts two years. That's a year longer than ours. I'm trying to imagine your inner engagement, intellectual inquisitiveness in finding the shortest path to perfection, the desire to make contact with the saints who have already traveled this path. In the biographies of saints everything flows smoothly and heroically, like the theme of happy lovers in novels. But in our quiet and monotonous life problems rear up at every step. The will is not accustomed to deference, it demands subtle explanations from the lazy and still undeveloped mind, and if it doesn't receive them, it can suddenly behave tactlessly, caustically, demand more logical reasons, which the spiritual guide can't provide either.

My greatest consolation at the moment is that in a few months I will begin my studies, the tenth and eleventh grade, and later philosophy and theology. As never before I am consumed by the thirst for knowledge, I want to know more precisely what lies hidden beneath the beautifully embroidered mantle of the Almighty. Why does the world that I am observing hold so many mysteries, and why can't I decipher them myself? Now even the monastic life of monks is a mystery to me. They bury their heads in the clouds, to better see God in the sky. But the God of monks on the stage that I now find myself on, is hardly perceptible, He speaks like a retired actor, as though headaches were tormenting him, He gulps syllables like half-chewed nuts. I strain my eyes to see Him better! I make my hearing more sensitive to hear His whisper, and all in vain! Perhaps I'm too dumb to respond to His action. My skin is too thick to have the life-giving rays of His sun penetrate it easily.

So I'm trying to get used to the routine of the hours, of the recited psalms, of the clang of the bell on the floor calling for prayer, of bending the knees and folding of the palms, looking at the monstrance, contemplating the Stations of the Cross, saying my prayers on the fifty-seven beads of the rosary. These activities are accompanied by my sense of loneliness, my bare feet wrapped in a long white wool robe, which with each motion arranges itself into ever different folds.

Before I compose a greater whole someday from the described fragments, I am now writing a diary, letters to my moth-

er, my aunt Irena, my brother, and Krystyna. Writing protects me from overblown memories, which, like a wild forest grow in my imagination in less than one evening. My "holy ladies from the suburb of Jasna Góra" wanted to know the secrets of life in the cloister, I can now send them bagfuls of notes, letters and disquisitions, which hatch in my head. I can impress them with anecdotes about anchorites and their caves full of dancing devils and harlots, trying to beguile the holy men into temptation. I can write about the miracles that are happening, and which the average mortal cannot see. I can write about the silence in the monastery's corridors, that bangs its bare ribs against the walls. Let them be entertained by the news that every Friday I scourge my shoulder blades and ribs with a whip. I can send them a few drops of blood on a small cotton swab in a letter. The female commanders, who sent us to the front lines, can see with their own eyes that the blood is real.

I do not know if you remember how our pleasant guardians wanted to be exemplary mothers to us, virtuous eligible maidens, a moral model for all occasions, Polish women faithful to Church and country. Aunt Estera, the eldest sister of my father, watching this group, said: "the shortest path from the village to the city leads through the sacristy." I guess she was right. We both ran away from the grey clouds over the fields, the deep pine forest with its wild animals, the dark abysses of dense shrubs, oaks and pines. It was this dark forest wall that separated your village from mine, where I spent several years during the war. I never had the courage to venture alone into the denseness of the forest. And I did not foresee that someday Providence would send us along similar paths for berries that we gather for our eternal life.

I ask for your remembrance and prayer,
Brother Modest (Marcin)

Thursday, December 13

I still haven't sent the letter to sister Florencja, I can only do so through Aunt Justyna. They are in the same mother-house of the congregation. Florencja is a novice and for sure her superior controls her incoming correspondence. After re-reading the letter, I see that I gave vent to bitter melancholy. The donkey on which I am galloping toward religious perfection, sometimes unnecessarily rears up its hind legs.

December 13

Dear Aunt,

After a long delay I finally wrote a letter to sister Florencja. It is frank, in a similar mood to yours in the letter you sent me two months ago. I am sending it to you and ask that you please deliver it. If my sister would want to write me back, I would ask that she send it to my mother's address. From time to time my mother visits me in the monastery and brings me correspondence. With cordial greetings and monastery beads,

Brother Modest

P.S.
A certain thought comes to mind, which I would like to share with you now. I do not understand why I can't be frank in my con-

tacts with sister Florencja, you and my loved ones who are partly responsible for my being in the monastery. I felt embarrassed to ask you to be my go-between in my correspondence with sister Florencja. We are united by similar goals that we both chose for ourselves. Writing the letter to her, I was completely honest, because I wanted to share my personal experiences. After re-reading the letter, doubts appeared in my head, that the Novice Master may not tolerate my statements, and sister Florencja's supervisor may have reservations about some of my wording. I am now trying to figure out how to reconcile family ties with the new rules and regulations of the monastery. Could it be that her being my cousin, and I her cousin, could stand in the way of our aspirations for perfection?

Friday, December 14

For the last two weeks we have been practicing Christmas carols and pastorales, under the efficient and tireless baton of Brother Longinus. I have little to show in this area. It turned out that with such moderate pitch I can barely be a figurehead in the group of baritones. After the initial selection we began practicing in small groups.

"Our Longinus has a temper" - whispers Brother Rufus into my ear, the tallest among us - "son of a farmer from Ostrołęka." Vocally and pitch-wise we were included in the same category, i.e. a group of rams bleating delightfully on a green meadow.

During the first attempt the Novice Master assisted us. But it turned out that Brother Longinus was able to cope quite well with us. He has a large-scale voice, he can sing bass and falsetto, and he plays the harmonium and the organ, and supposedly also the trumpet. For our modest needs he was a golden apple, which fell from the branches of Providence. The Reverend Novice Master was quite obviously pleased with him. In his five-year practice such a talent had not manifested itself before.

Saturday, December 15

The book by Little Theresa of the Child Jesus is getting more interesting the further I get into it. She imagines that she is a small child climbing up the slopes of Mount Caramel to holiness. She wants to constantly "look up to the Lord and place her trust in Him;" she wants, like a "little bird" to not change her place so she can be touched by the rays from the look of her Redeemer.

So far, I learned about saints by reading "Saints' Lives" by Rev. Piotr Skarga. His language and way of thinking, though very noble, strayed far from contemporary imagery. Therefore, the work by the Carmelite nun, written in simple language, with an admixture of monastic humility, is more easily absorbed by my mind. I inhale it like fresh mountain air, I feel it through my skin. I also like the form of the diary, written day by day.

At the recommendation of her older sister, in the Order of the Sacred Heart of Mary, the keeping of a diary was an act of courage and common sense. The notes -- written in the difficult period of illness, when tuberculosis was destroying her lungs, when she spat blood into little handkerchiefs, and when fever was tormenting her body -- could not have been disingenuous. In such a state additionally forcing herself to mental effort was evidence of her superhuman willpower.

Thanks to these diaries we have a genuine person, whose path to perfection we can track from day to day and treat it as a mature role model, despite her young age.

Monday, December 17

I do not know what happened to me last Friday. After shutting off the light and beginning the lashing, I was carried away by penitential feelings, and I began hitting my body with all my strength with the waxed whip. I assumed that I could surprise myself, my own skin, by making a decision that I normally would not have made. The executioners did the same thing with Jesus. That he did not rebel excited their surprise all the more.

The next day I could barely move. When sitting down and standing up during the breviary I clenched my teeth. Today in the bathroom, using a small shaving mirror, I checked my skin. On the thighs, abdomen and back it was still beet red. In three places there were stretches of black and purple welts. Luckily it's December and I can wear a thick flannel shirt. The spacious, soft tunic of the robe is now the best protection for me.

For the future I should have a little more common sense and humility, because such abuse of one's own body certainly does not lead to holiness.

Thursday, December 20

I am reading the first part of "The History of the Soul", that is, Manuscript A - dedicated to the older sister, Paulina, bearing the name Agnes of Jesus. The little Saint's statements are bold. She writes that God does not call to perfection those who are worthy of it, but only those whom he wants, or, as Saint Paul says: - "Is God unjust? Not at all! For he says to Moses, 'I will have mercy on whom I have mercy, and I will have compassion on whom I have compassion.' It does not, therefore, depend on man's desire or effort, but on God's mercy. " (Romans 9:15,16).

This was the text, if I'm not mistaken, that the German Augustinian Marcin Luther slipped up on, coming to the hasty conclusion that some Christians are meant for heaven and some for hell, regardless of the deeds of the particular individuals.

What I know about this subject comes mainly from the "aunties" my mother was friends with. I continue to have large gaps when it comes to theological knowledge. I could use a dictionary here of heresy or orthodoxy in the Catholic Church (or telephone contact with Aunt Irena or Krystyna). I do not want to expose my thoughts or my desires to a lack of orthodoxy.

As a young nun Saint Teresa of the Infant Jesus was doing quite well. How poetic the comparison is that "all flowers created by Him are beautiful, the splendor of the rose and white lilies does not take away from the fragrance of the tiny violet nor from the stunning simplicity of daisies..." Nature is rich in diversity and does not divide flowers into better or worse. In the flowery mantle of spring it is enough that I be a thistle, a barely tolerated weed. Its leaves, protected by small thorns, define the state of my soul.

Saturday, December 22

I should get down to writing letters for Christmas. This will be the first Christmas away from home. But touching paper reawakens memories, feelings, the singing of Christmas carols together by the Christmas tree and at Midnight Mass. In a group like ours, you have to disrobe from the feelings and sentiments as if you were taking off your clothes. Hide totally naked under the monk's robes like a featherless chick. Only the head and part of the neck can stick out, the rest of the body has to disappear, even the hands. Hands, fingers gesturing in the air, catching objects that don't belong to them, touching other fingers and the warm skin on them; caressing the wall in the darkness like a live animal.

I won't know now how to be too effusive in my greetings. What I would like to wish my friends may have no meaning for them. They live in a different world. I don't have the free space that they enjoy around them at my disposal, the white snow in the mountains and on the fields. I won't sit down together with them in the sleigh with the bells, I won't swish down the hill on my skis.

For sure I will be longing for home, when on Christmas Eve we will walk down the corridor single file to the refectory. Mother knew how to create a festive atmosphere. We sang carols by the Christmas tree; father would lead us in his baritone voice. There was always fish in aspic, herring in sour cream, sauerkraut and mushrooms, noodles with poppy seeds, Greek-style fish, red borscht with tiny ear-shaped ravioli, two or three salads, compote made of dried fruit, and the Christmas wafer for sharing. We would go to the neighbors with the wafer. One could hear the caroling throughout the entire apartment house. Everyone was in a good mood. Afterwards, we walked to Midnight Mass over the crunchy snow.

In the convent all intimacy of mood evaporates into thin air. There will be no gingerbread toys on the Christmas Tree, no colored-paper chains made at home by my brother and I, no tinsel, no hand-blown glass ornaments and butterflies. Grandma Maria used to say: "You really don't know what you're missing, until they take it out of your hand."

Sunday December 23
An almost festive mood. Immediately after recreation we practiced Christmas carols and the Gregorian Mass. The one voice Gregorian chants caught my attention. I had the chance to listen to that type of music many times on Jasna Góra. Now, I kept staring at the tiny

squares on the four lines with the notes and tried to hang my voice on them. For me the melody was missing a specific meter and beat, you could fit many sounds in one syllable. Our amateurish throats irritate Brother Longinus. He would like at least one or two voices in his choir to sound like angels.

We don't yet know the full charm of church music that he wants to initiate us into now. Irritated, he refers to the expression of Johann Sebastian Bach, that "he would trade all his works for the writing of one Gregorian Mass." The Gregorian Chorale is the most valuable pearl of early Christianity. It is the carrier of the religious traditions of the Jews, Syrians and of Byzantium. I look respectfully at the embarrassed faces of my colleagues, their strained throats, and sincere desire to make the music angelic. From the very beginning this music was meant for boys' and men's voices, in line with the recommendations of St. Paul of Tarsus that "the woman is to remain silent in Church."

Midnight Mass

During Midnight Mass we sang carols for various voices. Brother Longinus was in his element. I surveyed the faces of the faithful in the temple filled to bursting. There were many pretty women, but the delicate features and details looked fuzzy from the elevation of the choir loft. Everybody was in a good mood and everybody wanted to satiate their eyes with the extraordinariness of the moment. After some time the aroma of the incense burnt on the main altar made its way to the choir loft.

The Prior's sermon seemed a bit long, but it didn't have all the ascetic accents that the Novice Master's conferences had. It even seemed a bit too secular to me, too general, even though the Christmas season is an opportunity to recall the essential moral principles.

Brother Longinus played the organ during Holy Communion and we, one after another, down the center aisle, went to the altar to get the Eucharist. On the way back I tried to fill my eyes with the faces of the faithful, but I often lowered my eyelids, unable to hold up to the gaze of the young women or men. A lot had to have changed in my psyche over the last months. I am unsure of myself; little things spook me. If someone were to ask me about a mundane thing, I wouldn't know how to behave. Walking up the steps to the choir I noticed that there was a lot of shoe-carried snow at the entrance doors and only then did I feel cold, and yet the church had not been heated the entire time and during the singing of the carols I was able to see the cold-induced billows of my colleagues' breathing.

Friday, December 28
While reading the "History of the Soul" by St. Theresa of the Infant Jesus several questions arose in my head that I am trying to find answers for. First of all, if I want to become a saint, must I have talent, of the kind that out-

standing musicians have, or poets, or even gardeners culti-
vating plants? You can't be a musician if you are tone deaf,
but it is absolute pitch that allows a musician to faultlessly
recognize notes, specific chords and keys. Talent is a gift
that one is born with.

You can't give yourself talent, just like you can't
pour some of God's Grace under your skin, it flows down
from the heights. God as the independent manager of
the universe distributes talent and blessings according to
His sole discretion. All other consumers of oatmeal and
mashed potatoes can work at it 24/7, 31 days a month, for
the remaining days of their lives and they will never emerge
from the cellar of their foggy existence.

Over short spans of life I can manage to have sin-
less feelings, thoughts unsullied by anything perverse, I
can patiently endure pain, kill hatred toward the enemy;
but after fifteen minutes of existence in such a state of
weightlessness my little chapel of holiness collapses, because the foundations beneath it are not stable. My mind
undergoes natural scattering, which like mosquitoes bite
the smooth surface of concentration that it took so much
effort to attain.

A anyhow, is it possible to attain perfection with
a totally trained brain? The few monks who achieve that
probably have a ready plan, as if etched on the inside surface of their skull. God pulls them toward Him like a fish
on a hook.

Wednesday, December 31

The old year is fizzling out like a dying carbide lamp. I am bidding it a humble farewell only because it led me to the threshold of the New Year. In it I will try, as I had been in the final months of the old year, to forget about the past that I come from, in which my parents and brother are still rooted, in favor of a more rigorous asceticism, which perhaps will lead me to holiness. In the monastery I feel as secure as if I were in an armored bunker, though at times I would prefer that its walls would crumble in the morning.

Our holy patron desert hermits, Paul and Anthony, had an easier life than us. They hid out in the desert, far from the populace, in secret places meant for ascetics. They didn't have to worry much about love for their neighbor, about cooperation with colleagues as stubborn as goats. Lord, forgive me this aversion to my relatives, I come from a town that deals in devotional objects, tap water and bread from bread pans that wasn't thoroughly baked. From a town that badly treats its pilgrims. The iniquities of my countrymen fall on me. I have to repent for them.

Monday, January 7

Mother came to see me yesterday, on the feast of Epiphany. But before we saw each other, she spent some time with the Novice Master. I don't know what they were talking about. She was probably asking how I was managing in the school of religious life. Or maybe it was the Reverend who wanted to find out who had planted so many religious devotions in my head already.

I greeted mama very cordially. The Novice Master was very polite and praised me that I was trying hard to fit into the monastic style of life. Mother spoke very enthusiastically about her older sister Justyna, who has been with the Samaritan Sisters for 23 years already? Now the time has come for the younger generation – she added. She was thinking of my cousin and me. Looking at mother I thought: if she were an educator in a high school run by the Sisters of Nazareth or of St. Clare she would be persuading all the girls to enter the nuns' order. She is a born rabble-rouser. That I am here is thanks to her compelling inner strength.

She carried in herself the seed of many future religious vocations. Like a fish bobbing along in a warm harbor, she was full of gluey roe. All you had to do was rub against her, listen to her enthusiastic evangelization on behalf of religious vocations.

Mother brought me several letters, among others from sister Florencja, Janusz P., and Zygmunt H., and totally unexpectedly from my Latin teacher at Henryk Sienkiewicz High School. My letter to Janusz P. was very much to the liking of his parents. Janusz is also heading for the novitiate. If everything goes well I will meet him in eleventh grade in Cracow.

Mother was pleased that I had adapted well to the new life style. Nothing of interest had occurred in the environment I had left behind. My close friend Leszek Koper wants to become a cop. Our paths must diverge of necessity. When I joked: "Tell Leszek that when he learns how to catch perps and drunks well I will ask him to arrest all the devils in our monastery, which hinder us from our path to holiness," mother said sadly: I doubt that he attends church now. Leszek's father, who was a great patriot, would probably not have approved this decision."

Mother gave me a hand-knit sweater to wear under my robe and a pair of gloves. Also a supply of postage stamps. She suggested that I make contact with Brother Benedykt K., the sacristan, who will gladly help me mail my letters. While mother was still here I glanced at the letter from Sister Florencja.

Samaria, Niegów, December 17

Dear Marcin,

I was delighted at your letter. You broke your silence, which started to worry me already. The family treated my entering the Samaritan Order very seriously and practically nobody writes me any letters. Luckily, I have Sister Justyna, my aunt, nearby. Sometimes we get to take a stroll in the garden, sometimes we share news of family and relatives. I recently found out that Uncle Ludwik is ill, he stopped working in the factory. Aunt Helena takes very good care of him, they were always close. He was the dearest to me of the whole family.

After reading your postcards my head started buzzing. You are writing about things I have little knowledge of. And I always thought that as an older sister I ought to know more. Now I am jealous that after the novitiate you will go to college. And that in a few years you will become a priest. I can't have such aspirations. After the novitiate they will farm me out to some institution with sick children, or will make me a farm steward because I know farm work. After all, that is all I did with Dad. My life will be a little different from the life of my older sister Wanda, who already has three daughters and works her tail off with Władek, so they can make ends meet.

For me the novitiate is like a long unplanned vacation. Our mother, Rufina, the Novice Mistress, is setting up order in our heads. She is teaching us the principles of the religious life and care for others, especially the sick. She spends a lot of time with each one of us. There are eight new ones of us and seven from the prior year. Two already left. I think our novitiates are similar. We have frequent conferences, spiritual reading, and ways of the cross, novenas, rosaries. We also recite the breviary, but ours is not as long as the one the priests have.

Sometimes I think about our family, as one great religious vocation hatchery. Aunt Justyna showed everybody the way, and then I allowed myself to be tempted, then you. Your mother mentioned to Sister Justyna that your brother Janek is also making noises about going to the monastery.

I value the time I spent with you all. I often think of you as my brother. Because I was older I looked at you somewhat differently than a sister would. You were athletic, muscled like a young colt. When you used to kick the soccer ball around with other friends, I used to madly ride around the sports field on Janek's bicycle. Those were my happy months. Your and Janek's friends treated me very cordially. Give my best to aunt Irena and Mrs.

Krystyna. Thanks to them and your mother I have grown used to "asceticism." Now I see that never having been in a religious order, they were expressing their faith a little too noisily. Nonetheless I always think of them cordially and often pray for them.

Please greet and hug your mother for me. She helped me the most, when I came to Częstochowa and was somewhat spooked by the city. I also remember how sometimes we strolled by pond, by the now boarded up brickyard. You once gathered a bouquet of field flowers and gave it to me. I was then getting ready to join the order. I still have one blue cornflower, which I pressed between the pages of my prayer book. Whenever I look at it I pray for you or think of you.

My cordial greetings to you and please write, write often.

Sister Florencja

That was the only letter from the mail my mother brought me that I had wanted to read right away. I was not disappointed. My thoughts, like frothing bubbles in a bottle, were ready to shoot out of the top of my head. I quickly went to meditation, huddled into myself... Nothing interested me anymore. I just wanted to wake up anew in a dream that rapidly enveloped my body like w warm down comforter. Angels in heaven probably lay themselves down to sleep like that.

Dear Marcin,

Thank you for your extensive and detailed letter. I was curious about the details of life in a novitiate, because I am thinking ever more frequently about following in your footsteps. I can change the piano music to quartets, quintets and octaves of church oratorios as well as into organ pedal nomenclature- for the pedals under the feet. I am also thinking that we could prepare for the high school graduation exams together. I miss you now as if you were my own brother.

My best wishes to you for the holidays. Together with the shepherds in the Bethlehem stable and the angels I sing: Gloria in Excelsis Deo.

Greetings from my mom and dad,
Yours as always,
Janusz Potera

Janusz's announcement that he wanted to "follow in my footsteps" delighted me. We will be able to be together again. How strange it all is. I thought I was running away from my friends, because I didn't fit in with them too well. And they again appear on my path.

Dear Marcin,

I found out from Zygmunt H. that you decided to enter the Pauline Order. That in part explains your interest in Latin and literature. I am upset that I am only now finding out about your life plans. I was always well disposed toward you and watched how you struggled with yourself to get good grades. I only send postcards with greetings to my students. This time I am writing a letter believing that you continue to try to understand the world as it is, and not as you would like to see it. Nonetheless, the fact you are evading having to stand in line for meat, bread and sugar deprives you of contact with real life.

I am writing to you about this so that you don't delight in the justification that you are now free of responsibility for the fate of the environment that you left behind. Each one of us has to carry the yoke that history has placed on us. The monastery isolates. It is easy to get inebriated with asceticism, long fasts, neglecting one's own body. It is easy to "get sick at your own death" that Soren Kirkegaard writes about in such a scholarly way. But now we don't need any more "stiffs" we need new "resurrectors" who, like Christ, will rise from the death after three days, shaking off the dampness of the grave, the darkness of the cemetery silence, the sky constantly clouded over with historical events.

In moments of agitation, of lack of tolerance for his reforms, Luther threw inkpots at the devil, made him a bump on his bald pate, but he did not compromise his principles. We too should throw live coals straight at Destiny's eyes. In my opinion locking oneself up in a monastery makes sense, if at the right time you re-

turn from it and take up the battle with the ideology which is now poisoning the souls of our young people. The pinch of didactics that I'm serving up here for you is the result of my 27 years of experience in dealing with young people.

For the New Year I want to wish you a lot of satisfaction and common sense, which you can learn from the Roman classic while studying Latin.

Very cordially,
Ignacy P.

The letter from my Latin teacher is a truly moving and beautiful document. He not only didn't forget about me, but like a true teacher he always cares about my spiritual profile. This is just one more proof that the world that God created is beautiful, the people in it are good, and the stars shining in the sky praise the Great Non-Present One and give us additional energy.

December 21

Dear Marcin,
Best wishes for the holidays. It's been almost half a year since you disappeared. Our Latin professor was asking about you. I told him that you were hiding out in the dark Pauline Fathers' cellars. I must have said something stupid, because the professor got upset and was ready to roar. Our mathematics teacher, Mrs. Stefania, came back from her maternity leave. As usual she is making us work hard. After giving birth to twins she's half the size she

was before, but it's still too much, when you want to compare her with our girls, who parade airily down the boulevards and in the Park on the Third of May. We reminisce about you quite often, even though some pout that you were too secretive. Lucynka and Stefan say hi.

Be good and write,
Zygmunt H.

Zygmunt has many fine qualities and can be a fabulous partner in many undertakings. His conduct breeds trust and it is easy to get attached to him. I suppose that in a monastery he would lose half of those characteristics due to a negligible need to engage oneself in anything. Passive virtues are in fashion here, and humility most of all, blind obedience, purity and poverty, that is, getting by without things and objects that make life easier.

Thursday, January 10

During lunch and dinner we read aloud stuff that is instructive and didactic. On the whole these are lives of saints, their memoirs or books about missionaries. So far we have read the contemplations of: Rodritius about the monastic life (I remember the sentence: "The monk who does not mortify his flesh is as dead as a tortoise shell"), then John Cassian's "Collationes Patrum (about the dessert fathers) and currently "Philotea, or an Introduction to the Pious Life" by St. Francis de Sales. In addition we learned that its author is a doctor of the Church, the patron of poets, writers and journalists. As a young man he went through a personal crisis, having wrongly understood the doctrine of predestination. For some time he was afraid that he would go to hell.

We, the future clerics, have the responsibility of reading aloud. It is a painful experience for those who feel an aversion to public appearances. For the Novice Master, the Prior and others, who will be doing their evaluations of us toward the end of our novitiate, this is an opportunity to make observations. Some of us stammer while reading, others, not understanding the sense of the sentences, twist words, still others, with a monotonous delivery, put the monastic brothers to sleep, who are sluggish anyhow due to lack of physical activity.

As of Monday it's my turn. I will be reading "Philotea" for a week. The book was written with lay people in mind, who want to be on the path to sainthood. St. Francis de Sales' ascetic persuasions were written for the chosen and after so many years they adhere to us like well-tailored clothes. As a doctor of civil and canon law, and also a doctor of theology, he fields splendidly all questions that might arise during the course of the reading. It will take me many years before I learn how to deal with the limitless knowledge which this saint navigates so faultlessly.

Friday, January 11
I had a talk with the Novice Master. He wanted to know how I was coming along with my meditation. I felt that he wanted me to describe in my own words what I

was doing during the 30 minutes assigned to contemplation. I replied that all sorts of concentration, inner focus, were very much to my liking. I like to dive into my own thoughts. Imagination carries me along like a kite borne on the wind. Time passes quickly for me and I feel aversion to the next task that follows.

The Novice Master said that that is a good characteristic, it ought to be cultivated, but real meditation ought to help us reveal God and remove the obstacles that exist inside us. Our own dreams need to be eliminated and replaced with thoughts of God, Who is Truth, Life and Ultimate Goodness. One needs to be guided by the desire to understand the method used for hundreds of years by the desert hermits, harassed by constant pangs of conscience. One ought to learn how to bend one's nature to do that which it doesn't want to do.

Not everything that he said was intelligible to me.

January 12

Dear Professor,
Your letter brought me great joy. It was sincere and deeply touched problems that society is currently struggling with. If I gave you the impression that I am running away from life and communal responsibility, I can explain that I was never guided by such motives. The desire to enter the monastery appeared in me as if by chance. I lived near Jasna Góra, I was an altar boy, I knew a few of the priests and at a certain moment I desired to follow in their

footsteps. The same thing happens when somebody wants to become a physician, a lawyer or a musician. I came to the conclusion that I will attain more if I become part of a larger organization.

Now the whole difficulty is to become an integral part of the institution, which accepted me into its ranks. The teachings of the Novice Master make a big impression on my still very inexperienced mind. He inspires us daily with examples from the Old Testament, exhorts us to gain control over our own body and to do penance for the sins of others.

I am gathering the thoughts and energy in me so that at the right time I can be ready for work and service among my own countrymen, with whom I spent so many beautiful years. A long road awaits me before that happens. After the novitiate I have to complete some courses necessary for my high school diploma, after that two years of philosophy and four of theology. The possibility of further study excites me greatly. I am cognizant that I have a meager supply of information.

In the quiet of the monastery I have a lot of time to think through many matters anew, which I was barely conscious of just a few months ago. Today I better understand that I cannot hold the world responsible for being the way it is. I have to find a place in it for myself and measure life with my own measure, not push the blame onto others.

In conclusion I would like to mention the gratitude that I have in my heart for you, professor. Thanks to the Latin I learned I can now make better us of the Psalms of David, and I now better understand texts which have become my daily bread. To my utter amazement it turns out that church Latin is much easier than the Roman classics: Ovid, Horace or Julius Caesar. Reciting the Breviary day after day, reading texts from the Bible and the Church Fathers in Latin, I really have the opportunity to get acquainted with many forms of the language, of which you spoke in class, and which at that time didn't penetrate my head. I now look into the dictionary more eagerly and make use of available cribs, that is, translations of the psalms by Rev. Wujek, S.J. or even the newest ones, such as the beautiful one by Leopold Staff.

> *With deep respect,*
> *Marcin Kowacz*
> *and now Brother Modest*

After reading the letter I have the impression that I am constantly lacking the right words to form my own thoughts, I also seem to lack poetic inspiration, so the sentences wouldn't be so crude. I am trying to be smarter before the professor than I actually am. Could this already be that elusive insincerity that is sometimes ascribed to people of the cloth?

Tuesday, January 15

During the morning conference the Novice Master asked a rhetorical question: is there any sense to strive for personal perfection, poison one's liver over every petty offense? Why not settle for mediocrity, rye bread, and porridge and take it easy in the quietude of the convent?

Then with unprecedented rigor he said: we hid ourselves here, in St. Paul's hermitage, to load our batteries with spirituality, lighten our minds with knowledge and temper our wills for the fight with belligerent atheism, with all anti-Christian doctrines. We have to become twentieth century crusaders, march across Europe: from Portugal's Fatima to the Urals and from the south to the north, from Sicily to the North Pole. We have to convert the materialistic East and the West that has become secularized to the very marrow of its bones, bring Buddha to Christ, convince Leszek Kołakowski, God's personal enemy, not to waste his talent on proving the superiority of the atheists over the theologians.

After this inspiring conference it seemed to us that the white Pauline robes flapping in the breeze had set fire to the poplin suits, starched shirts and military uniforms festooned with medals.

Thursday, January 17

Last night I had a dream again. I unexpectedly found myself under an enormous mountain of ice. I was wondering why I wasn't cold. I was just in my nightshirt, barefoot; ice was melting under my feet. All around me there was a huge swarm of men dressed in black suits. Each of them carried a small silver anvil in his left hand, on which he rhythmically tapped out a very strange melody with a small gold hammer, which I had never heard before. Focused in on themselves, they did not pay attention to what was going on around them. On the slope of this mountain there was a scattered group of people, who bent their heads rhythmically down to their knees, pronouncing verses that I also could not understand.

I unconsciously felt that I was in a place where I shouldn't be. Looking around for familiar faces, I was mainly searching for the face of the Prior or the Novice Master, knowing that they would be unhappy, because I had left the monastery without their permission. Suddenly I noticed that the men in the black suits with the silver little anvils and the golden hammers were sculpting a statue of the devil in a block of black ice. It had an enormous head, like that of the Egyptian Sphinx, with its tongue hanging down to its chin, with teeth as big as apartment buildings, with enormous bat-like ears and eyes that emitted fire and sparks. I was petrified.

I instinctively reached for my rosary, but – dressed only in my nightshirt I didn't have it with me. I wanted to kneel, fall on my face, as the pilgrims do on Jasna Góra and beg God for help. But I realized, that in this place I would be doing homage to the devil, and not to the Creator, who made him and me out of nothingness. At that very moment I thought I heard a knock on my door. That was the "alarm-clock brother" walking past our door and calling us to meditation. I looked around; the room was pitch black, probably the middle of the night. No one reacted to the knock.

I thought that I was doubly dreaming and that if I didn't wake up from that first dream, I would be late to chapel in the second one and everybody would notice. I pinched the skin on the back of my neck and on my stomach. Nothing changed. After a while I noticed that two figures in robes were approaching from a distance. They had their hoods drawn over their heads. One of them on approaching looked an awful lot like the figure of the Novice Master, bent at the waist. In a split second I recognized the other, it was the Prior. They were coming straight toward me. My legs buckled under me. I knew that I deserved a reprimand and that they could now expel me from the novitiate.

Yet the faces of the approaching monks were very solemn, as during a concelebrated Mass with the bishop in the cathedral. They regarded me with a lot of tolerance. They declared that all three of us were dreaming the same dream. In their eyes I had been singled out by our patron, St. Paul the hermit, who, so as not to break his holy silence, often uses dreams, in order to teach us about important and decisive matters. The Prior asked that I look around me once more and note as many details as possible. I now saw that the great ice plain on which we stood was surrounded by an ocean on two sides. Straining my hearing I could even hear the sound of the waves hitting against the ice.

I noticed a moon clock on one of the clouds, which indicated midnight. The Prior – turning to the Novice Master – said:

"Please explain to brother Modest that we came here to witness Satan's funeral."

At the same time the men in black suits, with the silver anvils and golden hammers interrupted their music making, as if on command. It became dark and cold, a dry wind blew from the East, and lightning flashes broke against each other on the horizon. With a trembling voice, as if during confession in the confessional, the Novice Master said:

"The Holy Universal Church is burying Satan today, in the black depths of the Atlantic, in the coffin of the waters. Let all thought of him from this moment on die out, let him be sucked into the dark hole of non-existence for all eternity, for which we fervently beseech You, our Lord and Eternal God."

Automatically, as if I were an assisting acolyte, I replied:

"Amen."

The "alarm-clock brother" must have in fact passed by my door. Both my companions were already making their beds and snorting energetically away over the basin with cold water. I jumped up on my feet. The dream like a chimera kept appearing and then disappearing under my eyelids.

To this day I have no idea what all that meant. I had no desire to report such an odd dream to the Novice Master. I was unable to cope with that phantom all day long.

Friday, January 18

During the pre-noon conference the Novice Master opined that we should imitate our native saints. We almost have as many as the Italians or Spaniards. St, Stanislaus – bishop and martyr and St. Andrzej Bobola had shown heroism and an undaunted spirit. From the narration it followed that the Cracow bishop Stanislaus (about 1030 to 1079 A.D.) had a conflict with King Bolesław, because he defended the law and morality. The king tried to take away the estates that the bishop had acquired several years before from the knight Piotr. The estate had been transferred on the basis of a gentleman's agreement, i.e., on the basis of a word of honor, without any written documents. Knight Piotr had been dead for three years already.

In the difficult dispute with the family of the deceased, bishop Stanislaus turned to king Bolesław for a binding decision. The king, knowing that the witness was no longer alive, said that only the oral testimony of the witness could tilt the decision in favor of Bishop Stanislaus. In this situation the bishop went to the cemetery, fervently prayed at the grave of the dead man that he should come to his aid. Amazingly, the knight Piotr arose from his grave and together with the Bishop went to the court. The bishop won the case in court, but the king decided to kill the "biting traitor." The bishop decided to curse the tyrannical and godless king.

On April 11, 1079, when Stanislaus was celebrating Mass in the Cracovian church on the Skałka, the executioners arrived. The king personally attacked the church dignitary and struck blows at his head. He disfigured the face of the body quivering on the floor by cutting off the nose, cheeks and lips. The body, hacked into 72 pieces, was scattered all over the area by the soldiers. According to legend, the pieces collected by friends of the bishop immediately grew together. Only the index finger of the right hand was missing. It was found in a nearby water fountain, in the belly of a fish, which shined like a phosphorescent brooch. The missing finger also attached itself to the rest of the body.

The death of St. Andrzej Bobola was even more cruel.

Saturday January 19
We had a new housing rotation today. I will now be at number 18, with two brothers from the academy: Brother Fabian K. and Brother Pafnucy S. The former is probably the most jocular spirit in our group. He is somewhat on the heavy side, as he describes himself, with traces of childhood smallpox on his face. He has big, brown eyes, always carefree. Brother Pafnucy looks like a figure in an El Greco portrait. He has an elongated, ascetic face, thick jet black hair which even when he gets a crew cut still tightly cover his skull. He has a large meaty nose and mystical, emerald green eyes which cause me to look at him as if he were a saint.

But this saint doesn't have a pugnacious Spanish soul. He is a Slav, he behaves as modestly as a maiden, he is excessively polite and eagerly puts into practice all the recommendations of the Novice Master. I was delighted at this change. Brother Sylvan, with whom I had been living thus far, had already begun to oppress my subconscious like a hard-edged suitcase pressing on my back. Suspicious in typically peasant fashion, devoid of sentiment, he followed me around with his watchful eyes like a detective.

Brother Fabian is the antithesis of Brother Leon. He only suffers when he has to be serious, when he has to participate in the Eucharistic procession with a dignified look on his face. At every other occasion he cracks healthy jokes and he's cheerful, sometimes a little too coarse. I was able to notice that during our move. The first question he directed at me was:

"Do your feet stink, little brother?"
"Why do you ask me that, Brother?" I answered his question with another question, not knowing how to react.
Because Brother Xavier's in Room Number 7 smelled like rotten onions and I couldn't sleep."

Brother Pafnucy blushed to the root of his hair and rebuked Brother Fabian, that he might have offended me. But Fabian's face was so angelically innocent that I thought: "We will have a good time living together."

Tuesday, January 22
The Novice Master often quotes the old hermits, whose maxims are not easy for us to assimilate. Today he surprised us with a new portion of quotes: The reckless

monk becomes stifled by his thoughts, like wheat by thistle weeds or referring to St. Anthony the Hermit: My sons,
death is our apartment, the prison cell our place of residence or that we carry the body but our soul wants to
"undress" itself of the flesh as fast as possible, of that dead
and revolting clothing.

The Reverend Father is busy perfecting our souls,
but he doesn't always notice the sensitivity of our minds.
After each such ascetic reprimand I am unable to sleep
for a long time. I then try to reorganize things in my head
anew and I repeat after the psalmist:

> For Thou hast formed my kidneys
> And have woven me in my mother's womb.
> I praise you for how strangely I am created,
> For Your works so worthy of admiration,
> And you know my soul to its depths,
> My Being is no secret to you,
> When in concealment I was taking shape,
> When I was being plaited in the depths of the
> earth.
> (Ps. 139, 13-15)

Wednesday, January 23

It hurts me; the separation of soul from body gives
me actual physical pain. I am myself when I am in my body,
without the body I am an abstraction, a spider web on a
cloud, woven in my name by an ascetic spider. Punishing
the body with fire is torturing my soul. Without the body

my soul is blind, cannot differentiate between smells in the air, does not see colors, does not delight in tastes. Eating cauliflower gives me no pleasure.

Breaking a finger on the right hand doesn't hurt the hand, because physical labor is not in the sphere of its interests. It prefers bird down to polished furniture that you can sit or kneel on, to pray.

The soul, which does not delight in joy, which I feel when I delight in life, isn't worth God's salvation. God only saves those who know what they are doing.

Thursday, January 24

I feel a lack of personal hygiene. I am beginning not to be content anymore with just washing my face in the morning in cold water, touching the back of my neck with a cold damp hand, to smear the grey streak on it pressed into it by the woolen, sweaty collar of the robe. I don't see any of my co-Brothers washing their genitals with a damp washcloth. We will get used to the smell of our bodies. Some of the older Priests or Brothers emit an odor of the "forest floor" or of sweet bees wax.

Brother Fabian, whom I live with, directed his remarks about "stinking feet" at me with a big dose of humor. His feet are the noisiest at the moment when they are liberated from thick woolen socks. An invisible stench cloud hangs about in the room for many long, exhausting minutes. Only gray soap and a stream of hot water could remedy his advanced state of fungal foot infection. My nose and my watering eyes before I fall asleep bear witness.

Saturday January 26

Yesterday, after the lights were turned off, I listened how my new roommates were using the whip. Brother Fabian, after two hits on his rear end, began lashing the wall vigorously. He groaned while doing this like a blacksmith's assistant while manning the bellows. Brother Pafnucy didn't spare himself decent whacks on his already skinny back. I had the feeling that his piety, modesty, almost childlike honesty were radiating from him even in the darkness. I became very glad that we were living together.

My desire to maintain strict silence on Fridays has a chance of success with his cooperation. Brother Fabian, due to his crudeness and liberal treatment of everyday matters, will be a real thorn in the side to us. The desert fathers would have assessed this type of behavior as flowing "from a body overheated with drink and food and due to a lack of spiritual vigilance over one's thoughts."

Tuesday, January 29

At a conference the subject of Polish saints came up again. This time St. Andrzej Bobola of the Society of Jesus. I go to all the conferences with a note pad that is already half-filled. I write down remarks that seem worth remembering.

St. Andrzej Bobola did not particularly stand out day to day. His superiors noted that he was impetuous, showed impatience, was overly sensuous and sensitive, was very emotional. He was athletic and healthy. He had a good memory, but was no intellectual. He did not get a high enough grade on the ad gradum exam which would have qualified him to teach in Jesuit colleges. The correspondence between the General of the Order and the Provincial lasted for three and a half years before Bobola was admitted to the fourth vow (in addition to the earlier vows of poverty, purity and obedience), absolute obedience to the Pope.

But Bobola as a priest made his mark as an ardent preacher and effective missionary. The Belarusian population gave him the moniker "soul catcher", somebody who knows how to snatch souls in flight. He had a resonant voice, an excellent memory and a sharp wit. The poorly educated Orthodox clergy were scared to death of him. He easily refuted their mildewed arguments. He began all his missions with a fast on bread and water, he did lots of pilgrimage on foot, he reached far corners of human habitation that even God and the Devil had forgotten about.

In mid-May 1657 Cossack troops began prowling in Polesie (East European lowlands). These were fragments of Bohdan Chmielnicki's revolutionary army. They murdered and robbed "papists" and especially monasteries and Catholic churches. On May 16, 1657 a band of Cossacks arrived in Janów Poleski, murdering catholics, uniates and jews. Bobola, snitched on by the local population, was captured by the Cossacks near Peredywy and bestially murdered.

The Novice Master spared us the details of how Bobola's body was abused. Nonetheless I knew them from my uncle Andrzej's stories, who was particularly devoted to the saint. I knew that the saint was murdered in the slaughterhouse in Janów Poleski. They tried all sorts of tortures in him, that only deviates could think of. including stripping the skin off his belly and lower back, cutting off his fingers and extremities.

At night I couldn't fall asleep. I realized that I would never be able to exhibit the kind of physical endurance that St. Andrzej showed. My body is sensitive to cold and heat. My nervous system is all over the place like a spider's web. The example of this biography made me realize that the first hermits, fleeing persecution, also must have had sensitive bodies. They ran away because they feared torture. Probably none of them were good martyr material. Later, they repented for the rest of their lives for their lack of courage, because they dared not show up in their own communities.

Toward the end of their long lives in isolation among hyenas and jackals, some were forgiven their cowardice by God, who gathered their battered souls unto Himself.

An outing. Like a flock of sheep imprisoned in a corral, we ran out of the monastery and onto the open field in twos and threes. It was a sunny and very cold day. We drew the cold air greedily into our poorly oxygenated lungs. Our spines straightened up, our necks stretched out, and the eyes swallowed up the vast expanse covered with a thick layer of snow. The Novice Master, the main jogger, took long, ever longer steps, to cover as much distance as possible, to tire our bodies, grown slack due to lack of movement.

We marched over bumpy furrows on snow-covered fields, on barely visible meadows, over the blunt heads of outcropping rocks and paths freshly made by the feet of hungry wolves. Beneath that thick layer of snow the earth looked like a woman's naked body. It didn't feel right, wounding her skin with our heavy shoes.

After an hour of invigorating marching we made it to our destination, to a small glade sheltered by some pine trees from the south and by the slope of a rocky hill. We sat around, like blackbirds, in a semi-circle on the snow, on jutting rocks and on a pine that had been blown down by the wind. Suddenly everybody wanted to talk, shouting one over the other, singing out loud fragments of songs, whistling, tumbling around in the dry, powdery snow drifts, throwing snowballs without looking.

I thought – isn't this the purest ecstasy – being part of magnificent Nature. After the effort of making sacrifices, sense-humiliating asceticism, after solitude and inner torment, such joy, delight that one exists. Joy was exploding me from the inside, such as I had never felt before. My thoughts were my body, my body was the red blood cells of my thoughts. I was ready to strip naked in front of everybody and dance like a Dervish, fascinated by my ecstasy, and to ask God for my small Assumption into Heaven, harmonized with space.

It was difficult for us to think about heading back. We were on nobody's fields, covered with a white blanket of snow, almost two hours from the monastery. After some time the cold started seeping into our skin, we started back toward residential buildings. The Novice Master began reciting the rosary aloud. We repeated after him in a somewhat hoarse chorus. Every Hail Mary like a snow-covered little bird, flew off onto a grey cloud, lurking on the horizon.

Saturday, February 2

The Feast of Our Lady of Candlemas is very close to my heart because of my grandmother Maria. She attached great importance to having a candle at bedside in every house in the village. I often saw grandma putting a blessed candle into the hands of the dying. She believed that such a person's sins would be forgiven and their tortures in purgatory shortened. For her, Our Lady of Candlemas was the patroness of a good death.

Sunday, February 3

Today I couldn't wait to tell Brother Pafnucy my dream. On the occasion of the Feast of St. Paul the Hermit, which falls on January 15, we recite a novena for nine consecutive days. We call this celebration "Paul's Days." The faithful sing hymns with us in church, which narrate the life of the saint; the priest recites a litany and special prayers. I was already connected emotionally with these festivities when I was an altar boy. Maybe thanks to those memories, I had a dream the other night which I desperately wanted to tell someone.

I dreamed that, as on every Thursday, we went out for a walk. But the terrain we headed into was completely unfamiliar to us. Everywhere, as far as the eye could see, there was sand and a gusty wind was blowing. The Novice Master announced that this time he wanted to lead us to ancient Thebais in Egypt, so we could pay a visit to our patron, St. Paul the First Hermit.

The road kept getting longer. We waded through sand dunes, the terrain looked exactly like the Sahara Desert. Looking around I noticed that our robes were gradually changing into white fur, of the kind mice have, and our white scapulars were slowly changing into long mouse tails. The same must have happened with our eyes, because our whites suddenly turned pink and none of us could control our darting eye movement. The sun was about to set when we reached the hermitage.

The Novice Master ordered us to maintain angelic silence, to in no way disturb the quietude of the holy Hermit. In a cave which looked like our cells, but in which the walls were uneven, in spots convex, in other places concave, there was – one could guess – eternal darkness. We were barely able to see the old man on his knees with his arms raised toward the heavens.

At first I looked at him as if he were a statue carved in stone, which barely looked like a human being. His uplifted arms were so skinny that one could barely see the network of veins and feebly pulsating blood under his skin. That pulsation of the blood made me aware that this figure was alive.

I had no idea how this miraculous phenomenon, existing already for so many centuries, could suddenly be awakened, torn out of the ecstasy of watching things invisible to ordinary human beings. As if in answer to my fears and concerns, the holy old man moved slightly, then, slowly, like a wax figure, he turned toward us. His face was bony and emaciated, his eyes shone like live coals taken out of an oven, a long Egyptian nose and a wrinkled forehead, to which were attached two swallow nests of bushy eyebrows. His beard was thick, down to his ankles – it tightly covered his frail body.

Yielding to a stupid, monkish curiosity we scattered to all the corners of the cave, looking for invisible treasures, which the Saint had probably accumulated over the centuries: the texts of old manuscripts, which he no doubt knew by heart by now, prayer books, from which he recites his prayers, litanies to the dead that he buried with his own hands, papyrus rolls of the Old or New Testament. But the niches and cubbyholes in the walls of the cave contained nothing more than a few dry dates, coconut shells with the white meat inside, barely bitten into. I looked with terror in the direction of the Novice Master, who, watching this scene uncoordinated by him, was afraid that the old man's heart would break in a moment.

But the holy patriarch did not seem to be moved by our invasion. Nothing existing on the planet was able to disturb his forever-congealed concentration.

"I am no longer of this world," he whispered. "I am with the angels now, with the prophet Elias on the chariot of fire, among the saints of the Church Universal." Then, folding his hands in prayer he began to repeat:

"Oh Lord, protect me from the plague of little white mice with long tails, from their darting pink eyes, let them vanish in the desert coolness." After this prayer our ears, noses and hair began to grow back. We began looking at each other in embarrassment.

The sound of the bell out in the hallway suddenly tore me out of my dream world; I jumped up on my feet. Morning light was already making its way gently into our cell. I began dressing hurriedly, to make it on time to the chapel for contemplation.

Dear Krystyna,

When I am unable to keep myself in check, to control my imagination as it disperses to the four corners of the earth, I get down to writing. It is easier to sort through thoughts on paper, write words, divide them with commas or end them with a period.

In the monastery I am having a hard time controlling my bad moods. Supposedly nobody wants anything from anybody, but everybody, sulking, walks next to everybody else. Every few moments one has to rush off to seminars, not far, just the next floor down, not far off beyond the sea, just to the adjoining room. There can be a thunderstorm or blizzard raging outside, a high wind, to which I would gladly fling open the windows to chase the stale air out of the corridors, but the monastery walls are massive enough that they isolate us from the dangerous tempests outside the windows.

We trot through the murky corridors all day long, in the white-painted, small cells, from the chapel to the refectory, from the refectory to the chapel for the Angelus. Sometimes a bit of split pea soup or cabbage soup aroma reaches our nostrils from the kitchen, the sound of a bell in the corridor irritates our ears a bit. Often when I want to be alone, delight in some thread of my own thoughts, somebody tugs at my elbow, reminds me that we now have to gallop over to the conference hall. The Novice Master prepared a new lecture about hermits, who, suffering from a negative reaction to matter, have renounced everything that is mundane, which can favor their senses. They recommend that every monk plunge into the abyss of soundless speech, and never leave his cell.

You can guess that sometimes I rebel. I am too young, after all, to be embarrassed that I exist. For me matter is not a sin, it is a bundle of energy, a handful of sand, a slab of iron, a part of the galaxy. I barely became flesh, barely had my first erection, I already have to sprinkle my head with ashes like the hermits, squeeze myself into a crack in the soil, so as not to hamper the desert chimeras at the surface.

Dear Krystyna, in fact I still don't know what a soul is and if anything exists at all, aside from my consciousness. Yesterday during morning contemplation I puzzled over this problem and didn't come up with anything interesting. I don't even know what eternity is, and what the past and history are? Every day more questions arise than answers. Maybe I should apply cold compresses to my head.

St. Gregory of Nazianzus wrote: "in life there is nothing good without sadness in it." I think that a grain of melancholy has already started sprouting in me too. I am even bothered by the squeaking of the floor in the small labyrinth of the monastery, by the symmetrically woven spider thread on the ceiling, the lazy march of a centipede and the derision of the over-production of thoughts that I don't know how to cope with. Also the struggle with my body, which either is digesting something, craves something intimate or else constrains my desires by its overpowering sexuality.

Dear Religion Teacher, has the thought entered your heads even once, that in recommending me "to the safest monastic environment under the sun" you would evoke so much fear and terror *in my heart, bodily longings, which I can in no way satisfy. Maybe you will think that the wings of melancholy have carried me too far. Yet I prefer to mutilate the pages of my notebook with my steel-tipped pen than desecrate the murkiness and quiet of the monastery with a wild scream.*

Your barbarian Marcin,
Revolting against Brother Modest, the modest one,
Who queued up in the line to heaven with empty pockets
Behind the ruffians from the street, the melancholic and
the good for nothings.

Thursday February 7

I live with Brother Pafnucy in one cell, but there is never enough time for chitchat. We choose recreation time to gossip a little and share our impressions of various things we've read. He was recently fascinated by a book of exegesis on the subject of Lucifer. According to scripture the Archangel Michael cast him down from the heavens into the infernal depths. Why did both the great clans of spirits begin a war with each other in such an early stage of their existence? None of us knew how to answer that question. Brother Pafnucy thought that the reason for Lucifer's fall was a lack of obedience. The devils wanted to walk down their own paths from the very beginning.

It seemed to me that Lucifer was being blown apart by his own internal contradictions. He wanted to simultaneously be divine and reckless; he thought that he possessed all knowledge, and did not comprehend that the

143

created being must bow before the being that has eternally existed. God spread his peacock feather fan throughout the entire cosmos, not leaving much space for Lucifer.

Brother Fabian joined our conversation unexpectedly. And instead of discussing cherubim, seraphim and superior authorities, he started to ridicule the lame Polish devil Boruta, who had come to his village to the blacksmith to get his hooves clad in golden horseshoes. And every Saturday, in a black suit, black shirt, with a red bow tie under his chin, he would importune the ladies, who were looking for rich bachelors. One of them that our Fabian used to court gave in to Boruta's persuasion. They found her on Sunday morning in an ice hole with a straw noose around her neck.

We both had doubting expressions on our faces. Then Brother Fabian began to beat his breast and assure us:
"I adjure you on my grandmothers' health, that it's the pure truth!"
"But your grandmothers are probably no longer alive?" I joked.
"One is alive, and she's only 74 years old."
Then Brother Pafnucy began to tease Fabian:
"So you came to the monastery after you were disappointed in love?"
"What sort of love disappointment are you talking about? I couldn't get involved with a woman who had drowned. My father would have kicked me out of the house," Fabian added.
It was impossible to get bored in Brother Fabian's

company. I could have sworn that on his father's side he came in a straight line from the Zagloba, the Polish version of Falstaff. The laughing eyes of this cheerful fellow added charm to his words. May the angels gild him for the rest of his days.

Friday February 8

I succeeded in maintaining silence the entire day. During dinner I went with my plate to ask one of the Fathers for alms. It looked strange. For some time he seemed not to notice me. I waited for him to call a Brother over with a serving dish and only then did he throw a few pierogis with sauerkraut on my plate. In the evening, clenching my teeth in pain, I eagerly scourged myself with the whip across my buttocks and shoulder blades. My skin was sore; heat rapidly rose to my head. Nonetheless I had the feeling that Brother Pafnucy is much more eager than I, he lashed his emaciated body for an awfully long time. I felt sorry for him. Those were the kinds of lashes that fatso Fabian should have measured out for himself, but that one first whirled the whip around his head, cut the air until it whistled, next he beat his blanket with the whip, lashed out once or twice against the floor or the wall. It seemed that he was whipping an ox, not himself. After a while, with the feeling of having done his duty, tightly enveloped in his blanket he lay down on his mattress, preparing for blissful sleep.

I tried to sum the day up in my mind before falling asleep. But the devil, that tempter, quickly reminded me that part of my deeds was done for show. I wanted to impress my superiors, show myself off from my better side in the collective mirror. I wanted to debase others by showing that I was the more eager one, whose natural behavior could have been better received in God's eyes. Like a courtyard turkey I had made too much noise with my fluffed up tail.

"God, be merciful to sinful me."

Tuesday, February 12

The Novice Mater left for Jasna Góra to hand in our semi-annual reports. Since yesterday Father Roman is taking care of us. Thanks to this we have a little bit of freedom. At the ascetic conference Brother Fabian asked a question, which caused widespread consternation.

"Father, can the devil be saved?"

Father Roman, who gave the impression of being slightly stumped, blushed like a rose and sought an appropriate answer in his head:

"Of all creatures the Devil is the most accursed being. He is malicious, ugly and deformed. He is the antithesis of divine goodness, beauty and magnificence. SO how can he be saved?"

"And what about divine mercy?" Brother Fabian did not give up.

"Divine mercy is not unreasonable. The devil tried to ape God from the very beginning; God by saving the Devil would have fallen into his trap. He would be imitating a comedy in which the Devil was playing the first violin."

"And can the Devil convert and repent for his sins?"

"The fall of Satan was greater than the fall of our parents Adam and Eve. Original sin, through which humanity became a prey of hellish forces, was wiped out by redemption, but Satan's sin can never be redeemed. The dogma about the eternal curse on Satan cannot be revoked."

It was quite a while since we had such an off the beaten track kind of ascetic conference. Father Roman was now red, now pale. He probably thought that he had ventured too far in his argumentation. Truth doesn't need so many words. What's the use of enlightening novices about dilemmas that have not yet been fully explored by theology? He happened upon a stone rolling under his feet, which Brother Fabian undoubtedly was.

I had to mentally agree with Arsenius the Hermit, who stated: "the talkative monk is stifled by a waste of words like wheat by weeds." We had the feeling that we had sinned because of uncontrolled speech and questions that we were asking like preschoolers incompletely affirmed in the faith.

Friday February 15

We go to confession at least once a week. Some of the more eager ones among us go every two or three days. In going to Holy Communion every day we have to care for the purity of our consciences. Being 24 hours a day under a common roof, prayers and meals spent together cause us to knock against each other like bottles in a tight box. It would be best if we all believed that we are empty milk or holy water bottles. God forbid that we'd be empty beer bottles or bright cream-colored wine bottles.

We lead an open life, so every slight offense shows up black as coal on snow. I ponder how it is possible to pursue perfection in such conditions, without falling into a sterile routine?

Compliance with regulations that date their beginnings to the great Fathers of the Church: St. Basil, St. Augustine and St. Benedict, the dramatic experiencing of liturgical rituals and symbols – all that inclines us, boys from the village and a few from the city, take take up various paths to perfection. A lack of adequately developed imagination and natural weaknesses result in our meager accomplishments. In our skimpy space at a breath's distance from each other we step on each other's heels and make room with our elbows. Our trainer's encouragements to ever greater effort just cause us to keep trotting ever faster – in place. Close to exhaustion we approach the goal line very slowly.

Monday, February 18
Father Kayetan Boręcki, the Definitor (a clergyman who is the official advisor to the head of the monastery), arrived from Oporoof. He is an adherent of severe discipline. There were rumors that he adds ashes to his food, wears a hair shirt made of horse hair on his bare skin

underneath his robes and often fasts on bread and water. He had also exorcised the devil two or three times from possessed women in Opatoof and on the Skałka in Cracow. In his opinion the new crop of religious vocations is tainted with Marxism and secular culture. That is why he advised our Novice Master to really sift through what he has, and get what's left moving faster. He likes to repeat:

"A decent monk is one who believes in God the Father, prays to all the saints and waits patiently for the resurrection of his sinful body."

We were all panic stricken. In the choir loft, during breviary prayers, everyone tried to read the parts assigned to them as accurately as possible. When a Latin word was mispronounced there was a knocking on the bench, which up to now had never been practiced. After the matutinum and the examination of conscience we returned to our cells, meek as lambs. Everybody was glad the day was over.

Wednesday, February 20

Lord, protect me from myself. I stayed for several minutes more in the choir loft after Vespers. I had to pray, I did not know that Father Kayetan was sitting in the last bench. As I was leaving the choir loft he called me over with a wag of a finger. He wants to see me in his cell in ten minutes. A cold sweat bathed my skin. I must have committed some infraction, or somebody ratted on me or – perhaps – he doesn't like the way I walk.

After knocking on the door to the guest cell, in which the Definitor was staying, I heard after a long pause:

"Enter."

Father Kayetan was sitting behind his desk, slightly bent over his papers. His grey, bushy eyebrows and hazel eyes deeply set in his skull made an impression. He was apparently reading my thoughts, because he indicated with his eyes a chair that was standing to the side. I sat down on the edge and nervously buried both hands in the sleeves of my robe. Father Kayetan remembered me as an altar boy at Jasna Góra. He was curious how I was getting along here. After this mild question I shot out like dumb Jack from his sling shot:

"Father Definitor, I like everything here: the quiet in the hallways, the regular daily routine, the variety of personalities, the recitation of hymns in Latin and the instructive conferences of the Novice Master. But I am nagged by doubts whether I really have the calling? My aunt and first cousin are Samaritan Sisters. I have a very religious mother and I keep wondering if their pious attitudes didn't become mine. And I wouldn't want to cheat God."

"Dear Brother, don't worry about it. Whether you have the calling or not will be decided by your superiors. If our order of hermits will need you to fulfill its plans, then God and the Divine Mother will shower you with gifts and graces. You don't have to eat delicacies and marzipan for breakfast to be a good monk. A handful of barley or beans is enough. You will learn on your deathbed if your stay in the monastery was necessary for your salvation or not. "

"So I will never have any certainty?" I stammered

"And what do you need certainty for, Brother? Faith in one's calling is not necessary for salvation. A true monk, incapacitated by the three vows: of obedience, poverty and purity, will never be certain of his reason or his salvation anyhow, nor that God will look kindly on his labors. He should just go straight ahead, like a horse with his blinders on, not counting on any reward in heaven or on earth. True love of God is blind, just like the effort of the farmer who throws the seed into the soil in the Fall."

❧

February 15

Beloved Son,

Thank you so very much for your last letter. I'm happy that you continue to trust me and aren't ashamed to share your fears with me. I have as many of them as you do. I ran away from home when I was fourteen. I was suffocating in that crowded cottage. I had five adolescent brothers and three younger sisters. Two other sisters from the first mother and three brothers were part of our family too. The adolescent boys' abusive jokes drove me crazy. The young people from the village often visited my brothers and sisters, it was sometimes really packed in there and a little too unruly.

I wasn't at all attracted to the prospect of working in the fields and around the farm buildings. So together with a younger friend, Valerie, we planned an escape to town. We were both young, pretty I suppose, hungry for adventure, after finishing elementary school we set off for the world. We slept the first few nights at my older sister Leokadia's place in Więcków. Valerie knew how to sew, so she got a job in a clothes factory. I found a job in the parish. I helped Josephine, the sister of the pastor, in the kitchen. In September the pastor sent me to the Sisters of the Resurrection High School.

Those were the most beautiful years in my life. I studied, supported myself, and devoured books. The pastor was like a father to me, I learned a lot of good things from his sister. The quiet and orderly life in the parish became complicated with the arrival of the young priest Krzysztof Szarotka. That was his first job after graduating from the seminary, and he wouldn't leave me alone.

After graduation I decided to look for another job. I went to Łęcików to my friend Antka, who had been living there for a year already, had a job and a boyfriend. I went to the parish office. The pastor was a distant cousin of my benefactor from Więcków. He gave me a job without any problem. I helped Serafina in running the kitchen, as also in the parish office. My work and my personal contact with the housekeeper and the pastor were quite okay. The rest you know, I told you many a time.

I fell madly in love with a guy who worked stocking the fish hatcheries. We were planning to get engaged. My jealous friend, who was infatuated with Alek, tried to break us up, telling me that Alek betrayed me with other girls and that I would never be happy with him. Bitter and rebellious, after three weeks of acquaintance with your father, who in the meantime came to paint the parish church – I decided to marry him.

But the memory of my first love weighed on me in my later life. I was no longer able to be entirely happy. That is at least what my thoughts kept whispering to me. At the moment of your arrival in the world a new feeling sprouted in me – I became the mother of my first-born child. The mother and only the mother. My love for you already existed when I was carrying you in my womb. Beloved Son, forgive me these sudden disclosures. Sometimes it is easier to convey on paper what would be difficult to communicate by word of mouth. My past is the beginning of your life. I don't want and don't see any reason to conceal my past from you and I think that in the future you also will have nothing to hide from me.

Your very loving,
Mother

This letter made a big impression on me. I did not know all the details of my mother's life. It also followed from it that I continued to be connected with her ambitions and life desires. She is treating me like an adult earlier than I deserve. She took my entry into the novitiate as an adventure equal to her youth. Wounded by the early failures in her own life, she wants to save me from all possible mistakes. Or maybe save herself and forget about the past?

Saturday, February 23

In the choir loft I sit on the fourth bench from the front, second from the left. In front of me there are three benches for the brothers who are lay members of the convent. We look at the shaved heads, the naked ears, the short and skinny necks, the freckles and the birthmarks on the skin. I have the feeling that "my rear" amuses my neighbor sitting behind me.

For three days I have been watching the spider that began weaving a web where the wall meets the ceiling. He has plenty of time; he's not hurrying to go anywhere. He plans very carefully, his thinking is precise, and he probably has an appetite for a fat fly or a centipede. Today during vespers I noticed that the web was shivering, a gray moth with a heavy body landed on it. The spider approached his victim without haste, allowed it to jiggle its feet around a bit more, spread its wings to their full span and like an experienced surgeon with one stab of the needle he let its warm blood flow into his hungry throat.

After the ample meal he took a nap, or maybe he just pretended to be napping and in his tiny brain planned another fine-woven net, in which he will trap his next victim. He will probably be successful. It will suffice that like Blaise Pascal in his manuscript, he will draw out several straight lines diverging in all directions, into an infinity unlimited by anything. Geometricians are able to do it, so is a spider. So far he has outwitted them all, he knows how to capably weave patterns on a dry branch, in a corner near the ceiling, without the benefit of a blueprint.

I wonder how the spider deals with its loneliness? Does crawling along monastery walls bore him, and his presence alone in the air suffice? How does he perceive our comings and goings, silent sittings in the choir loft, recitations of the breviary and quick exits from our benches to get Holy Communion, the long prayers of thanksgiving? Then he is alone again like a hermit, weaving the riddle of his life with his threads.

I read with horror in one of the Fathers of the Desert that he tried to compare Satan to a huge spider and that the sticky devilish cobweb can entrap "saintly rogues, wise men sinning with the follies of their thoughts, frustrated bureaucrats and peasants, coquettish ladies and prostitutes and everybody who is tossed about by anxiety, profound loneliness and the illusions of this earth."

Sunday, February 24

I am note too sure how to get down to writing a letter to Florencja. I think about her often, maybe even a bit more intimately than a monk ought to. The months since our separation have only embellished her figure in my imagination. In sum these are very strange feelings, on the border of sentiment and attachment. Sometimes I begin to perceive her as a woman. Yesterday, during confession, I had the need to disclose "that I think about Florencja too much." The confessor probably thought that I had the Italian city Florencja in mind, and he dismissed this revelation with an obtuse comment.

Dear Florencja,

Sorry to have taken so long to answer your letter. Right after reading it I felt a strong desire to argue with you, various descriptions that you had used circled about in my head. I was even astounded that a small detail suddenly takes on dramatic form in a monastery, and a separation of several months is like a tragedy. So I had to restrain my heart and allow time to somewhat cool down my first feelings. As you probably already found out yourself, many thoughts and emotions too visible on the face can be concealed under a monk's hood. The feeling, with which I could embrace you like a hot wind, is now forbidden to me. The Fathers of the Egyptian hermitages always threatened a sentiment for women with eternal damnation.

Dear Florencja, so I nurture my soul with the same Lenten vegetable of ascetic recommendations which are probably served at your table, for the good of eternal salvation. What ensues from them is that we have to forget that we have a body, that we long for love, that with our senses we can experience a joy that the angels couldn't even dream of.

The impractical spirituality of monks is and always was a frolicking of time with eternity, a risky game for eternity beyond time. Meanwhile none of us is capable of renouncing what we are biologically and physically. Our past is in the tissue of our present. That we are attached to each other just increases the possibility of surviving in the world's chaos. Also only our intimacy can be a model for our closeness to God. God and the world are in us to the same degree to which we exist in the visible world and in the womb of God whom we cannot touch with our senses.

As you can guess, these are the trends of my daily contemplations...no doubt dented by the feeble words and the as yet undefined capabilities of my mind.

With, as always, a vivid memory of you,
Marcin

After a careful reading of the letter I came to the conclusion that I shouldn't send it now. Let it lie low in my drawer a bit still.

Monday, February 25

After the weekly confession I freed my head of the thoughts that had been defiling my imagination. At one of the conference I found out that "all sinful thoughts may be more deadly than physical acts that are not accompanied by full awareness." For monks who are working toward inner perfection, and that is what we are here for, the temptation to plunge in to a stream of impure thoughts is very great. The body like a hungry dog constantly reminds us of its needs. Our senses, hungry for sensations, provoke our lips, our teeth, and the taste receptors on the tongue. Even a dill pickle can cause us to get lost in its taste, forgetting that it is just a side dish.

Our awareness is not as pure as the air and cannot liberate itself from the material energy particles that pulse in our blood. It carries itself like the atom of the world reflected in a mirror. It can morph into a violin string, tightly stretched, that angelic melodies can be played on. That string may break when stretched and squeal piercingly like a stepped on monstrosity.

I tried to confess the offenses running through my head to Father Walerian, who dismissed me with the remark that the Guardian Angel was throwing huge blocks of ice into the boiling kettle of my sufferings, to cool down by hot interior.

As penance repeat the litany to the Guardian Angels three times.

February 21

Dear Son,

I am not in the best mood these past several days. Ugly weather, now snow, now rain and now a thaw. I often go to the Miraculous Chapel of the Blessed Virgin Mary and pray for you. Lately I've taken to the altar with the crucified Christ. You often served Father Justin at Mass at that altar. I think about the sufferings of the Divine Mother standing under that cross and together with her I pray for you. You are my crucified Jesus. The vows which you will be soon taking will be the three nails that will wound your feet and hands. I am pained that it is I who with my vow of giving you up to a monastery carved this cross out for you.

Janek is improving in school. I noticed that like his father he has a gift for drawing. His notebooks are filled with paintings of birds' heads, bears and foxes. I wish it were spring already. The firing up of the stove irritates me, by the smoke in the house and then by having to air the apartment before going to sleep. Together with aunt Irena and Krystyna we talk about hermits as we used to, and now also about you.

Cordial hugs,
Mom

Friday, February 29

I was unable to handle the contents of my mother's letter all day long. A poem arose from my inner dialogue:

My Mother of Sorrows
When we enter the foyer
Your tears are bigger than yesterday
Than in the landscapes of previous pain.

And yet you are not a mountain
Propping up rain-laden clouds,
You are not a bitterness-filled rose.

You are just my mother,
So why then, mother of sorrows,
Do you stand beneath the cross –
When I am no son of God?

Monday, March 3

During the afternoon conference the Novice Master again spoke of the devil – the tempter. It can take on various shapes; it can become a wolf, a rooster, or frog or a woman. It appeared before St. Pahomius as a lewd Ethiopian girl, to tempt him into sin.

In certain female convents the devil changed itself into lettuce so the nuns could eat it. Then it tickled them from the inside into the sin of indecency and self-satisfaction. Devils run through monastery hallways taking on the shapes of rats without tails and they bite monks to irk them into anger and dissatisfaction. The perversity of the demons manifests itself through their desire to drag all of us into the hell of their loneliness, total hopelessness and lack of love.

Wednesday, March 5
I have to boast to my Religion Teacher that I found some material about hermits. I am slowly catching up to her in knowledge that she accumulated during her studies. I would be very happy if I could become her equal partner in discussion.

March 7
Dear Krystyna,

I am delighted, because I found a manuscript in our monastery's library titled: "Dialogues of Fathers of the Desert." It appears from the introduction that one of our Fathers translated several books from the Latin from the "Gerontikon", or the Book of Old People, that you had mentioned in your letter. The book contains the remarks of St. Anthony the Hermit, The Abbott Arseni-

us, the Abbott Zacharias, John Cassian, Abbott Lucius, Macarius the Egyptian and several other famous hermits.

I finally understood that none of them wrote a big book, with the exception perhaps of John Cassian, and other hermits passed between themselves by word of mouth the more interesting happenings and utterances worthy of remembering. Their short biographies are appended to the translated dialogues, the so-called apothegms. I found out that Anthony gave away his inheritance, gave his sister away to a virgins' convent, and himself went out into the desert and took up residence in a grave. Abbott Arsenius was ordained a deacon, he was to be the tutor of the sons of Theodosius the Great, but despite this he "escaped from people" and went to live in the desert. Abbott Zacharias separated from his wife and leaving her with their daughter, left with his small son for the desert.

As you see, dear Krystyna, I am not wasting time and I am trying to get my nostrils used to the dry winds blowing from the caves of the hermits. It is still five months to the end of the novitiate, I hope that like the desperate sparrow I will make it to the first oasis, then to the fifth one and the tenth one and I will become one of these anchorites who tamed the desert sands, wild lions and palms. I suspect that if I found myself once again "in the world", that is, outside the monastery, my sensitized feelings would come across freezing winter winds. I would feel like a wild man from the Sahara suddenly deported to the North Pole.

With cordial greetings and requests for your prayers.
Marcin

Wednesday, March 12

I do not know why the Novice Master is against us using the texts from the "Golden Legend" written down by the medieval Dominican Jacob de Voragine. After reading the introduction and several biographies I became eager to get to know the entire book. From the legend for St. Paul the Hermit's Day I learned the reasons why he ran off into the desert.

St. Paul witnessed the capture of two young Christians, of whom one was "smeared all over his body with honey and exposed to the hot sun to be bitten by flies, spiders and wasps." And the second "was placed on a soft bedding in a delightful corner, and tied down with ropes that were concealed with colorful flowers, so that he could not defend himself either with his hands or his feet. There was a young girl there, very beautiful, but shameless and she began to act lewdly with the young man full of God's love. He on the other hand, when he felt his body reacting against reason, bit off his own tongue and spit it in the face of the shameless hussy." St. Paul horrified at these methods applied by the persecutor Decius, decided to immediately leave for the desert. There amidst the hot sands, far from the hustle and bustle of the world and the vulgarity of the persecuting Caesar, he could immerse himself in prayer and meditation.

Thursday, March 13

There was a snow shower early in the morning, but instead of snowflakes, a fine-grained farina tumbled forth from the clouds. When we went out for a walk after dinner the ground under our feet was soft. There was no trace of the snow. One had to wrap oneself tightly in one's coat, because the damp cold seeped into our bones. As usual Brothers Sebastian and Bogumił trotted at the head of the elongated file. I marched with Brother Pafnucy. Somehow we couldn't get a conversation going. During the march we were unable to fit into one rhythm. I had the feeling that I had to goad him to speak with each subject I brought up for discussion. He smiled, was pleasant, and also as boring as unsalted herring.

The only thing that constantly fascinated me was his naturally ascetic, elongated face. He could have easily posed for a painter for a portrait of St. Jan Kanty or the young Jesuit St. Aloysius. When he lifted his eyes upward it felt appropriate to place lighted candles by him or to try to place him on a field altar. I guarantee it, many passersby would have the desire to kneel and pray in front of so spiritually elevated a figure. Too bad that filmmakers, looking for original actors, don't look into the monasteries sometimes.

We were walking too sluggishly; the Novice Master and Brother Silvanus were catching up to us. The latter was giving a long-winded disquisition on how to tear up poison sumac by the roots. The Novice Master was clearly not betraying any interest in gardening. From that subject he quickly jumped to a topic much better known to him, the apparitions of Our Lady of Fatima and the need for praying for the conversion of communist Russia. It was well known that he gushed with missionary zeal to convert unbelievers, and his prayers for them oozed from his lips like, for many, saliva at a richly laden table.

The topic lasted for the rest of the afternoon and for intentions while saying the rosary on the way back. We all prayed for the conversion of Russia, a huge country contaminated with materialism.

Saturday, March 15

I know by heart the prayer of St. Bernard to the Blessed Virgin Mary added to the Litany of Loreto. When thoughts scatter in different directions like frightened sparrows, I then silently repeat fragments: "it has never been heard that you abandoned someone who came to you for protection, I stand before you, a crying sinner, deign not to spurn my words."

From my spiritual readings I learned that St. Bernard was a hothead, difficult to live with. He liked to order people around, lead, force through his point of view. But when he spoke from the pulpit, crowds gathered. Some of that pious insistence remained in the prayer: "O Mother of the Word, deign not to spurn my words, but listen to them graciously and hear them out." I would like to eat at least one handful of poppy seed from his bushel of piety. In his times there were fewer cynics in the world and it was easier to become a saint.

Monday, March 17

I hate to admit that I'm a dawdler, but today I hid in my cell to avoid work in the garden. I preferred to read the Treatise on God's Love by St. Francis de Sales than to get my hands dirty. Suddenly I heard a knock on my door and Brother Basil appeared. He scolded me like St. Michael scolded the devil, called me a lazy city boy. With lowered head I followed him to the garden. The dry branches had to be cut off the fruit trees. It was enough that I gave two or three blows with the machete and my thumb, the same one that was wounded with a splinter a week before, began bleeding profusely. The cut was quite deep, but Brother Basil didn't make much of it. A bit of iodine, cotton, a Band-Aid, and that's it.

My "humility" suffered the most from that. I was worried what others would think about my laziness. Brother Basil had an uncurbed tongue and that same day everybody knew about my attempt to avoid work.

Ash Wednesday

The following text from the Book of the prophet Isaiah made an impression on me: Shout at the top of your lungs, do not stop! Raise your voice like a trumpet. Closing my eyes I tried to imagine the prophet with a lion's mane, stentorian voice, and dry, sunburned skin. He must have known how to out-shout animals and people. Scriptural texts often taste like dried plums that have been lying around for some time. You have to chew them for a long time in your mind before they again begin to ooze some juice.

You have to fast amid quarrels and disputes and amid beatings with wicked fists. Do not fast as you are doing today, that your tumult should resound on high. The Novice Master, smearing the ashes on our foreheads, was a miniature prophet who leaned his tussled head out of the reading designated by the Church. None of us wiped the ash off for the entire day. It made a big impression on me.

Up to now Ash Wednesday had never made such an impression on me. I used tog o to Mass at church with my mother, but I would quickly wipe the trace of ash off my forehead, because I didn't want anyone in school to notice it. Here in the monastery, I better understood the meaning of the symbol and of the words spoken during the liturgy: dust thou art and to dust shat thou return. Ash Wednesday begins the period of Lent, Great Fast, a time of penance. The breviary texts are saturated with a mood of sadness. In the noon-time prayer, before dinner, again a warning: Days of penance have come upon us, so we can do reparation for sins and save souls.

Friday, March 21
During the morning conference the Novice Master reminded us that the Church, and in actuality the Order, is ready to receive our commitment to dedicate our life to God. We are to understand this in the sense that only the church authorities, and in the Order only our superiors are able to evaluate the credibility of our vocations and discern the invisible guidance of the Holy Spirit. That we

reported to the Order of our own accord is not sufficient.

I do not fully agree with such an interpretation. For me the vocation is more closely connected with the environment near the monastery in which I grew up. My older altar boy colleagues joined the novitiate quite often and there was nothing heroic or unnatural in that. That is what Romek Wojtasik and his brother Stefan, and later Maciek Rasiej and Franek Gorzki did. If someone had asked me then who I want to be, I for certain would not have wanted to be a blacksmith or a plumber. Wearing a white robe and climbing up into the pulpit in the chapel was very attractive to me.

Monday, March 24

The Novice Master often refers to John Cassian and the conversations with Desert Fathers that he wrote down. It turns out that this saintly writer, thanks to numerous journeys, had the opportunity to visit many famous hermits, among others the great Macarius the Egyptian, Moses the Negro of Ethiopia and Evagrius of Pontus. They made a powerful impression on him. The conversations, written down years later, are one of the fundamental works on Western asceticism. In Constantinople St. John Chrysostom ordained John Cassian a deacon, who in his old age settled in Marseilles, France, where he founded two monasteries – one for men and one for women.

Our spiritual guide loves to quote from the apothegms, that is, the pithy pronouncements of the Desert

Fathers. I was able to note down some of them:

Since I became a desert hermit, the sun has never seen me eating.
Arsenius, flee from people, and you shall be saved.
Mind you never introduce somebody else's words into this cell.
Humility is the crown of the monk.
Never eat with a woman.
It is a great thing to pray without getting distracted, but an even greater thing
It is to sing psalms without being distracted.

The day after the Apocalypse only the meek and gentle of heart will get to see the Face of the Lord.

Tuesday, March 25

Selected quotes from ascetic books:

It would be best if they cut off our ears and noses, and our hair, just like they shaved it off in the first week before the enrobing. From the back our heads look like poppy pods in the field. Each one is filled with poppy seeds. The seeds spill out easier, are obedient and submissive.

The stubborn monk who is an individualist, is a great calamity for a monastery. You cannot plant humility inside him, which is a most beautiful purple flower, spreading angelic fragrance throughout the monastic refuge; nor obedience, which is the only herb that heals the pimples of devilish pride on the skin of ego.

After supper, for forty-five minutes, we practiced the Mass by Palestrina, an Italian Renaissance composer. The texts are written in Latin, and scored for four voices. Instead of a soprano and an alto we have two tenors and two basses. We will sing the Mass in the choir loft in Church, during Easter. Brother Longinus is our conductor. I love to watch him suddenly stop being an affable novice and become a demanding concertmaster. Even though he has small square hands and short fingers, he waves his baton around quite handily. It can be deduced from his eyes that music is his enchantress and his inspiration.

Following his example I would like to learn something that is unique. Thanks to which I could develop my mind, and simultaneously give my feelings the opportunity to show what they can do. I suppose it's a beautiful thing to know how to tease life with the help of some ability, which dominates in us and makes our time more pleasant.

Thursday, March 27

I had the dumbest dream that a shaven novice's head has ever had in this monastery. It seemed to me that our senior, Brother Basil, came up to my bed, tugged me by the ear, and ordered me to get up at once and crawl around on all fours. Flustered, I muttered under my nose:

"But don't I have to put my robe on?"

"Have you ever seen a donkey in a monk's robe? Take my shoes in your teeth, we will go around the monastery. I heard that somebody is trying to get into the pantry next to the kitchen."

He quickly stuffed his pants belt between my jaws, pulled hard, and stuck his heels into my sides as if they were spurs. I felt his fat rear end on my back. My knees and arms started moving rhythmically by themselves. In one second I turned into a hairy donkey. The stinking shoes tied together with shoestrings dangled from my neck. In a minute we found ourselves outside the monastery. It was dark and cold. Silent, disciplined and obedient I galloped along at a small trot.

In order to tease me a little, Brother Basil pretended to be looking for my tail on my butt. The tickling and pinching forced me to quicken my pace. Suddenly, instead of to the garden, he directed me into a little road with Palestinian poplars growing on either side. The sun, like a huge yellow balloon lowered down from the sky, lit up the roadway.

"Listen, you incorrigible moron, Palm Sunday is beginning in an hour or two. You have the best, the only chance in the world to be a donkey on which the Lord Jesus will ride into Jerusalem. I had to train you a little, sober you up from your dreams and teach you politeness. After all, you will be carrying the King of Israel and the King of Mankind on your back. I am giving you this chance but remember, don't pick a fight with me," said Brother Basil, after which he continued, " I can knock those straw ecstasies of yours out of your head, just like you pop a cork out of a bottle. In the monastery you will never know for sure where real life begins and where dream looms. Walk more carefully on the ground than the Lord Jesus walked over the sea. After every day of frustration, doubt or despair, the memory of this event may be your only hope."

After waking up I stayed in bed until morning, completely bewildered and irritated. I wasn't sure if it was my raging imagination that was ripped into shreds, or the stench from the devil's nostrils that penetrated my skin while I slept.

It is already late afternoon, we are going to evening contemplation in an hour. The dream keeps bothering me. Not because it was so abysmally stupid, but that it appeared in my head at all. I am irritated by the fact that I have no control over my subconscious. I know that some sort of bacteria is hiding inside it, but I am unable to remove it. It evokes a near-feverish state in me, spooks my thoughts, which I would like to have under my control. Are such dreams a sin, for which I will have to bear responsibility? Who sowed such nonsense in my head? Why is monastic life playing such nasty jokes on me?

Friday, March 28
During the Way of the Cross I tried to take in mentally all the details of that event. I was most irritated by the scourging of Jesus. The torture of the live body of a

mature man by the executioners! The behavior of the person condemned to crucifixion could not be provocative in any way. Christ did not make threatening gestures with his fists toward the Pharisees and archpriests, he did not try to demolish the temple in Jerusalem, nor did he incite against the Roman occupier.

Why were there volunteers among the soldiers who wanted to weave a crown of bramble thorns for him? At the very thought of such a crime I felt my skin too tight on me. From the text read at every station it appeared that Christians continue to scourge and torture the body of Christ, committing sins and crimes.

After supper there was barely enough time for two of Palestrina's songs: "Crux Fidelis," and "Adoremus Te." I sang first bass, next to Brother Mark, who kept elbowing me whenever I fell off key. Brother Mark sings solo parts, and then every note in his throat vibrates purely and melodically.

Tuesday, April 1

A stroll in the garden. Hot rays sear through the scattered clouds. I am thirsty for their warm touch. I am delighted that the sun is licking away the remainder of winter off me. I share these thoughts with Brother Matthew, who with his eyes keeps looking diligently for something in the garden, jumping from one branch to another. His parents have a farm near Radom. He knows better than me how the twigs on bushes awaken from their winter sleep, and the winter crop sown in the autumn and the flowers in the garden awaken.

Then without any kind of introduction he begins talking:

"Father kept us in the fields from March until October. There was always a lot of work: plowing with a horse-drawn plow, weeding, sowing. I only had a younger sister, so everything fell on my shoulders. In the morning I also tried to assist our Vicar at Mass. Once I complained that I don't have time to do my homework, I keep sliding by at school from grade to grade on C's. He advised me to report to the seminary. There I would have plenty of time for study and I wouldn't have to worry about food and clothing.

"My friend Jarek, who had already written a letter to the Pauline Fathers and asked to be admitted, advised me the same thing. My father was furious, said that just when harvest was coming up I was "running away on him from the scythe." I felt sorry for him, but the desire to escape the heavy farm work took the upper hand."

I was deeply moved by his story. I returned mentally to my childhood spent at my grandmother's in the countryside during the German occupation. We started flipping through memories of haystacks; hands tying sheaves of rye and barley, digging for potatoes and grazing sheep on yet unplowed stubble. The recreation hour went by so fast that both of us wondered what happened with the time. Like wind that you try to catch in a sieve, it dispersed in the memories.

Thursday, April 10

During supper I tried to mentally transport myself to the Upper Room where the Last Supper took place. I instinctively directed my gaze to the main table, where the Prior, the Novice Master, and his assistant, our Confessor Father Walerian and the Father steward sat. The food was Lenten, beet soup made of beets alone and herring with potatoes. And for dessert apple compote. Despite this I had the feeling that we were over-eating.

At home during Holy Week mother used to feed us plain cabbage soup, hard boiled eggs, bread with marmalade and whey. Potatoes in their skins with sour cream tasted like a royal delicacy. Today I was filled with the feeling that in the Order every meal can be treated as a festive one. In the refectory the only persons present are the priests, the brothers and the novices who are candidates for proclaimers of the Good News. Sooner or later we will all go out into the world as apostles. I looked at the Prior with the hope that he would get up and tell us what an important moment we are experiencing today. Christ in the presence of His disciples performed the transubstantiation; He transformed bread and wine into His body and blood.

There will come a time that I will try to understand this mystery of faith in theological terms. Today is it enough that I can experience it with my heart, engage my feelings in it. The fact that Judas was also present in the Upper Room and that his act of betrayal toward Christ constantly repeats itself in the Church, filled me with fear. Statistically only one in two candidates will remain in the Order until death. The other half will be swept out of the monastery by life, which will subject them to bitter trials, overwhelm them with experiences beyond human strength.

Good Friday

I read the legend for the day of Christ's Passion, but instead of the story about the long and painful Way of the Cross on Golgotha, the author of the Golden Legend focuses mainly on the biography of Pontius Pilate, who allegedly was the son of King Tyrus, born of the daughter of a miller named Pila. Consumed by jealousy as a young man he killed his younger brother who was more talented than he. Condemned to death, and then pardoned by his father, he was sent to the Romans as a hostage. Rome, on account of his cruelties, gave him the management of the island of Pontos, whose population would not tolerate any authority over it. Pilate fulfilled his task very well.

In the meantime Herod, having found out about his resourcefulness and ability to handle his subordinates, made him his lieutenant with authority over Judea and Jerusalem. Pilate quickly made his fortune and made contact with the Emperor Tiberius behind Herod's back, thus gaining the Emperor's confirmation of the work he had already accomplished. For this reason there were some sharp misunderstandings between Herod and Pilate.

Meanwhile the ailing Tiberius finds out that a great miracle worker and healer, Jesus of Nazareth, is active in Jerusalem. He orders that Jesus be brought to Rome at once. Pilate, after having handed Jesus over to the Jews for crucifixion, panics, supposing that he will lose Tiberius's favor. By chance Volusianus, the Emperor's emissary, meets Veronica, who tells him about Jesus' crucifixion and shows him Jesus' image imprinted on the veil.

Volusianus takes Veronica to Rome. The Emperor orders the road to be covered with silk cloth for the reception of the miraculous image of Christ, and having looked at the veil, returns to health. He then orders Pontius Pilate to be imprisoned for condemning an innocent man to death. Pilate, expecting an ominous sentence, commits suicide, running himself through with his own dagger. The corpse was tied to an enormous millstone and thrown into the Tiber River, but unclean spirits, delighted with the evil and unclean body, tossed it now into the water, now into the air, causing a flood, and thunder and hail in the air. The people, unable to endure such afflictions, threw him into a mountain well, where to this day, as the legend says, demonic forces keep toying with him.

After supper we practiced singing the Easter songs: "A Merry Day Came Upon us Today," "Lay Down Your Troubles," and "Rejoice O Heart sore People." Brother Longinus was nervous, he complained that we were singing too mechanically, like recruits let out of the barracks. Probably because Brother Mark had a sore throat, sniffled and his vocalization wasn't even partly as clear in tone as always. On the other hand Brother Felix's tenor stood out, it seemed that he wanted to fly off like a lark from amidst the group of hoarse sparrows.

Holy Saturday

All the crosses in the chapel and the church were covered with violet cloth. From His death on Goof Friday to Easter morning Christ lived in limbo, spoke in that dark prison to the spirits locked up there who had shown disobedience against natural law even from before the Deluge. Christ the Redeemer also suffered for the unjust and wanted to lead them all into His father's house.

In an exquisitely beautiful, ancient homily for Holy Saturday we read: A great silence enveloped the earth; a great stillness and emptiness was on it. A great silence because the king had fallen asleep. The earth became frightened and grew silent, because God had fallen asleep in human flesh, and had awakened those who had been asleep for ages. God died in the flesh, but moved the abyss. He goes to find the first man, like a lost sheep. Those first lost people were Adam and Eve, the parents of all of mankind.

In the breviary next to the homily it was not noted who had first delivered it, a deacon, a priest, a bishop or the pope. But every word of it, emanating divine inspiration, seeped in through the skin, even skin as thick as mine. I often repeat with emotion: The earth became frightened and grew silent, for God had fallen asleep in human flesh.

☙❧

After the afternoon and evening recreation we had rehearsals of Palestrina's works which we will perform during the Mass at the time of the "Kyrie, Eleison", "Credo," "Sanctus," and the "Agnus Dei." Brother Longinus corrects the imperfections, has us do frequent repeats. The Novice Master listened patiently, did not make any additional comments. His ear is no better than mine. During a sung Mass one can hear the wavering in his voice, the unnecessary prolongations or divergences from the melody. The prior is much better in this regard. During High Mass he can give melody to each word and recite it appropriately. Even the exclamations. With my voice I wouldn't dare perform next to him, even as an acolyte.

Sunday of the Resurrection – Easter
The breeze of a Nature awakening from its sleep is blowing in the air outside the windows. Juices are nurturing the budding branches. The awakened sprouts of seeds are growing out of the earth. Together with the resurrect-

ing Christ they too are coming out of the earth, gathering themselves unto the light. I would sometimes want to fully comprehend the mystery of Jesus' resurrection. That His tortured, scourged, profaned, hung on the cross body, and His javelin – pierced heart rose from the dead – that He turned out to be the Son of God.

In the liturgy for today a triumphant Alleluia is heard everywhere, Christ having risen form the dead conquered death, will never die again. Alleluia. Death has no more power over Him. Alleluia. With full concentration, with closed eyes, I could listen to every musical phrase which composers have written to the syllables of that one word: Alleluia. One can plunge endlessly into the flood of melodious fugues and toccatas by Bach, Beethoven and Mozart, catch the tiny nuances, the loud note contrasting with the quiet one, place the refrain from a psalm next to baroque ornamentations. Music is a glorious hymn to Him who created the lark, the clouds and the blue firmament.

Tuesday, April 17

The novitiate in large measure is a school for molesting one's consciousness. I am unable to say it adequately, but I feel it with my skin. Our spiritual guide evokes phantoms in the mind, frightens us with Satan, teaches us lack of tolerance for our own body, induces us to fasting, to lashing the buttocks and ribs, to sexual abstinence There is a determination in him to take us apart and put us back together inside out. What was white in our life, must be dressed in mourning, joy and pleasures must be suppressed because they lead to sin.

He helps us tame our nature at the moment when for many of us life is just beginning, when hormones are just waking in our loins, the imagination opens up like the petals of the tulip to the sun, the world tempts with its variety, the cosmos with its enormity. The reprimand that we shouldn't eat ourselves silly because the more fat under the skin the less space there is for God's grace, doesn't always seem reasonable to us.

Eating three meals a day is contrary to the principles of the first hermits, who ate once a day, and some of them every second or third day. There were even those who ate only once a week. I wonder if hunger can cause hallucinations, the hearing of voices and seeing of apparitions. Death by hunger may be pleasant, because the body dies out gradually, loses strength, sleep comes which becomes pure dream.

After the Easter Mass I took a few coals from the Thurible, knelt on them, to crush them. I then added them to my coffee or soup. That ruined the taste of the dishes, but I was happy that I could mortify my flesh.

Saturday, April 19
Today during the spiritual reading, on the basis of what St. Anthony said to his disciples, I understood that the body contains an innate energy in it, which does not act if the soul does not wish it to. Our mind does not ac-

tivate itself, if the soul neglects it. There is also another energy, which flows from the nourishment and warming up of the body with food and drink: this is where the heat of the blood comes from, which stimulates the body to act. Nonetheless St. Paul the Apostle admonished: "Don't get drunk on wine, because that leads to licentiousness." And Jesus in the gospel commands His disciples: "Take heed therefore of yourselves, let gluttony and drunkenness not burden your hearts."

There is still a third energy, known to God's warriors, that flows from the traps and envy of Satan. Evil spirits often appeared in the life of St. Anthony, they led him into temptation, tried to defile his pious thoughts or provoked his senses by arousing the concupiscence of his body. Then Anthony would throw himself into thorns and brambles, to fight the aroused passions with physical pain. He chased the devils off and humbly gave himself up to the protection of the angels and the Blessed Mother of the Savior.

One of the main principles that St. Anthony recommended to young monks was constant residing in their cells. He liked to remind them: like fish that die when they lie on the shore too long, so also monks who delay returning to their cells, or get into discussions with lay people, lose the power of concentration. So just as the fish has to get back into the ocean, so we have to return to our cell: so that, having been outside too long, we don't forget about internal vigilance."

Wednesday, April 23

I don't write letters to my father too often, he was always a mystery to me. I try to imitate him sometimes, but I know that I won't be successful at it. I am unable to do the kind of work that, done by his artistic hand, amazed others. I remember how he renovated unpainted rooms. He began by pulling out nails, filing holes with plaster, evening out the walls. He often removed the plaster so thoroughly that he would leave clean bricks, which he then painted with a disinfecting and corrosive liquid to kill off the vermin. Finally he would take in hand a heavy horse hairbrush and begin to paint. Before beginning to paint he would check with the owner about the color of the paint for the primer, the designs and stripes next to the ceiling.

Sometimes, according to the customer's request, he would cut out special designs of flowers, grape leaves, bird feathers. He was proud of the fact that he alone in the entire town could do that. He considered the use of ready made designs on rollers cutting corners. After he finished a job it was difficult not to be delighted at the artistic work of the craftsman.

Sometimes I dream that with his tiny horsehair brushes, which he used to paint ceiling paintings, he would conjure up new interiors for our monastery. On white walls he would create a Fra Angelico angel announcing the birth of Jesus to the Virgin Mary, or the resurrection of Christ from His grave in the style of Piero della Francesca. The naked walls would not be standing idle; there would be something to satisfy the eyes and heart.

My father as an artist is able in a portrait to bring out what is hidden inside the person. Just as he did when he was painting neglected walls, he could also plaster over all the defects, holes punched out with a hammer when hanging paintings, cracks due to the age of the building. Most Holy Madonna, he could even layer on so much white, pink and yellow paint on my skin that I would shine forth in the monastery's hallways like many a saint.

Saturday, April 26
Recently I have been having headaches quite often. A dry pain, sometimes very acute, appears above my ear on the right side of my skull. It disappears unexpectedly, only to sit down again behind the ear like a stray wasp. I don't think that my constant struggles with my thoughts could have any sort of connection with this. Nonetheless the pain intensifies especially when all the noises die down and in the pin-drop silence I hear the rumbling of blood flowing through my veins.

Sunday, April 27
I pick legends from the Golden Legend, legends, that have a connection with our Order. The name of St. Mary the Egyptian on April 4th led me once more into the desert. As it turns out, she led a severely disciplined life for 47 years, in total isolation. We have information about her only because the Abbot Zosimas walked across the desert from time to time, trying to find some hermit. One day

he saw someone who was walking around stark naked, was black and burned by the rays of the sun.

It was Maria the Egyptian. At his sight she fled, but Zosimas began running after her. When he caught up to her she said: "Abbott Zosimas, why are you pursuing me. I cannot turn my face toward you, because I am a woman and I am naked. But give me your cloak, then I will be able to look at you without shame." He was greatly amazed when he heard her calling him by his name. And when they began to pray together with hands uplifted to the heavens, he noticed that she was floating almost half a yard above the ground.

She told him how she went from Egypt to Jerusalem to worship the Cross. But some force was pushing her away and did not allow her to go inside the temple. She asked the Blessed Virgin Mary for her intercession and promised that in the future she would renounce the world and preserve her purity. After a moment she was able to worship the relics of the Cross without any obstacles. Before leaving the town she bought three loaves of bread and some vegetables. A hidden voice said to her: "If you cross the Jordan you will be saved." She crossed the Jordan and wandered off into the desert, and those three loaves and the vegetables served as her food for many years.

Before parting with Abbott Zosimas she asked that he return in a year on Holy Thursday to the Jordan and bring her the Body of Christ. When a year later she saw him on the other shore, she walked on the water with her feet, cut up in the desert, and most eagerly took the sacrament of communion. When a year after that she did not appear again at the Jordan River, Zosimas went to pay her a visit. She was no longer alive. So he began to dig her a grave in the sand, but he soon tired. Then a lion appeared and dug up an appropriate hole. After that it disappeared quietly as a lamb. The deeply moved old man buried the saint in the sand and started on his return journey, to tell his brothers in the monastery about these miracles.

Wednesday, April 30

I am beginning to understand the mentality of certain hermits. Many of them abandoned their family homes to go into the desert and there spend the rest of their lives one on one with God. The ordinary mortal is frightened by solitude and monotony. Time becomes drawn out in solitude; the wet pall of melancholy clings tight to the skin like wet clothes. The sadness of transience gnaws its way into the bones like saprophytic bacteria.

From day to day, from month to month, from year to year their souls ripened in the dazzling glow of the sun m during sand storms, in the penetrating cold of the night. They traced the rotation of the planets in the sky, the flashes of angelic lights barely visible to the naked eye and God's face not wrinkled by time or transience. They were in possession of herbs that bring on visions, they talked with the animals. To those who wandered in the desert they passed along venerable mysteries, foretold the future. Many of them, without using a talisman or an amulet had power over demons. Were it not for their deep humility they could have blown the planet to smithereens.

April 30

Beloved and Dear Mother,

    You wouldn't even be able to guess what is currently occupying my head. I read a lot, almost everything that's in the monastery's library on the subject of hermits. Sometimes I have the feeling that sand is seeping between my fingers and out of my hair. Just several months ago I did not have the foggiest idea about them. Now I know that this was a very distinguished group of people. They escaped from civilized life into the wilderness, often with one book to read, which was the Bible. They recited several psalms daily. They read the four Gospels, the Letters of the Apostles, and the Apocalypse. After many years they almost knew these texts by heart. Their statements were like quotes taken straight from the Bible. From my readings in the refectory one sentence has stuck in my mind, that when Dostoyevsky was deported to Siberia, he also took only one book with him: the New Testament. Thanks to this he became the most Christian writer among the Russians.

    If my brain were x-rayed today, there would be more biblical verses in my head than the secular ones remembered from school. In the monastery you can be saved faster than out in the desert. Our spiritual guide exhorts us daily to work for perfection, sweeps secular images out of our heads along with the secular way of thinking. Frequent confession acts like a warm soapy enema. Living in one herd we don't have to be afraid of loneliness and they don't just feed us with herbs and chicory here. It's more like in the army – buckwheat groats, potatoes and noodles in all sorts of varieties.

Some hermits suffered from indolence and melancholy. The devils were all over them like wolves on a lone lamb in the field. Here in the monastery something is happening all the time, we go for strolls in pairs, we can't spend even one whole day outside the enclosure. Sometimes I can't believe that it is still possible to read newspapers, be interested in politics, the economy or sports. You can do without all those things in the same way that here we are able to do without pepper, cinnamon and pots of gold at the end of a rainbow.

Mother, you haven't written in quite a while, I'd like to see you. During Lent we practiced many songs, which during Easter we will sing from the choir loft in church. Thanks to these rehearsals I finally understood that I don't have a good ear. And I thought I could sing like Dad. Brother Longinus, our conductor, assigned me to the baritones. I envy him his beautiful voice. His Adam's apple takes on the look of a Turkey's gizzard when he sings. All he needs is a pitch pipe to intone each sound. I wonder if Janek has Dad's voice or mine.

I hid here in the chapel behind the altar to write this letter. Through the little window I see the main altar in the church and the figurine of The Blessed Virgin of Leśniów. She is as beautiful as the fairy tale Snow White. And she holds the Child Jesus on her left arm, differently than all the other Madonnas in Poland. Sometimes, when I feel sad, I come here to say the Hail Mary and I cuddle up to her just like I would like to cuddle up to you. Mommy, I have one more piece of news. For some time now I've been having headaches, in the area of my right temple. I go to Brother Basil often for the "Little Rooster" headache powder.

Aunt Irena probably still maintains contact with the Municipal Hospital on Polna Street. Could you organize some of that powder for me through her?

If it is possible, see you soon,
Marcin

I probably worried Mother with that letter. She is very sensitive inside and has an excitable imagination. She'll run with this to Father Eusebius, her confessor. Irena and Krystyna will know about this right away. But if I don't write, and something serious should occur in the future, they'll twist my head off. May heavens' will be done.

Sunday, May 4

We often recite the litany to the angels. The confessor reminds us that one has to ask for their protection, because they are guardian spirits, fighting in our stead with the devils. Looking at the painted images of angels, I see in their countenances the face of little girls or the faces of spoiled teenage girls. Their pink feet peek out from beneath their Raphael-like attire with toenails painted like nymphs. Heads in an aureole of corrugated curls, modestly bent, they remind me of phantoms flitting about against a background of clouds, rarely noticeable amidst real objects.

In the Bible angels accompany known figures in their personal events and everyday problems. The Angel

Gabriel announced to the Blessed Virgin Mary the immaculate conception of her son. Lucifer, knocked down from the heavens, was run through with a lance by the Archangel Michael. There are plenty of them on the pages of the Old Testament and in the biographies of holy desert hermits. Regiments of Seraphim and Cherubim, scattered all over the sky by the generous hand of the Creator, sparkle every morning in the rising sun like diamonds.

Being pure spirits they do not take into consideration the evolution of imperfect matter. They don't overload their heads with the particulars of transient things, they possess perfect knowledge and available at various levels.

What I am writing here is full of defects. All I know about angels is what I managed to read in our library. And what the Novice Master says about people "possessed by the devil."

So the question arises, why can't monks allow themselves to be "possessed by angels"? Become semi-hermits, so they would scream less, commit fewer sins, be half-angels, so they could more effectively and quickly approach perfection. Then their words would be as pure as spring water, it would have the power of praised gold, and they would not rust before they reach the ears of pilgrims hungry for divine enlightenment.

Dear Mom,

Your name day is this week. I won't be able to bring you a bouquet of fresh lilacs, as I have done every year. I know how much you love their fragrance. What I have an abundance of here in the novitiate, is words. During the day we have to maintain silence, so they gather in me like white down. I can breathe them, paste them all over scraps of paper, color them with ink; and those that are the closest to my heart I can try to use to write you a greeting card. Let some of them be like blue cornflowers, others red as poppies in the field. May still others be tawny-orange like butterflies. Some can be brown so they can remind you of Boletus mushrooms, which we used to gather together when you came to visit me at grandma's, or with an admixture of yellow, so they will have the scent of apricots.

The colors I remember from Dad's palette, which he used to present to his female clients before painting a room, are: saffron, pink-violet, turquoise, gleaming like the scales of a herring and coppery-green that is reminiscent of the roof of our basilica in Częstochowa. Do you already feel the fragrance of the letters and see the hues on this card? I would like them to be as alive as a branch of violet lilac that has just been touched. In April and May, when Nature awakens to life, may Spring burst forth during your Name Day in all the hues and light up your days. I wish you lots of good health, serenity and joy.

Always loving you,
You son

Friday, May 9

The sensitive monk is the one who is frequently tormented with pangs of conscience" I don't remember the occasion, when this maxim got stuck in my memory like a nail in the heel. Probably during one of our spiritual guide's conferences. It fits him like twine fits into the sole of a shoe; it fits to the train of thoughts that monotonously flow from his lips. In order to deal with it, in order not to consciously stifle tormenting pangs of conscience, I often tried to listen in on myself, quiet down all external, distracting noises and hums. I slipped through from one dark chamber of conscience to the next – even darker and duller one.

Flipping through the files of my imagination, page by page, I did not come upon any steam-spewing geysers of sin. I was afraid to tell my confessor about this, so he wouldn't think that I am leading an immaculate life. So I would write my sins down on little cards, and actually minor offenses that I happened to commit. After a week there were ridiculously few of them. I would add others, the kind that could occur, if I were less cautious. In the end, when you go to confession, you have to somehow impress the confessor. In the confessional it is sins that count, and not naïve confidences and showing off with good deeds.

So I reflected on what mortal sin is, and what venial sin is. Mortal sin for the angels meant revolting against God. I haven't the slightest reason to revolt against Him. He created me out of nothing, showered me with gifts. I can enjoy the sun and move over the face of the earth I am in the novitiate so that I can get to know Him better. With an attitude like that in fact you can't commit mortal sin.

The fact that I did not study moral theology and don't know all the distinctions between one sin and another should not evoke any additional anxiety in me. The time will come when I will rise to the challenge of the subject and open myself up to grace, which usually accompanies those who seek true enlightenment. I will do everything not to commit the blunder that stems from neglect.

There are sentences in Holy Scripture that awaken concern. We read in a letter of St. John: "There is sin that brings death." Then I don't know whether I am to listen to my own reason, which is looking for order in things, or else to my heart, which is guided by feelings, anxiety and fear.

From the teachings that I am getting here it appears, aside from the definition of sin, that the life of a monk must be ripped apart from within with the claws of conscience. The monk who does not hear all the most delicate whispers of his conscience cannot become a saint. Just like someone who is deaf and dumb, who is incapable of singing the beautiful melody of the Szymanowski's Stabat Mater.

Now I am worried that for the last couple of weeks my conscience has stopped bothering me. And I am worried that I carry in my body a dead mole which has stopped rummaging about with its little claws.

Tuesday, May 13

Yesterday before I fell asleep the headache returned. I tossed from side to side for a long time. I didn't have a "Little Rooster" to soothe the anguish. I must have mumbled something, said something nonsensical in my sleep, because both my companions were looking strangely at me while we were getting up in the morning. Yesterday I noticed with concern that during the monthly haircut, the rattle of the hair trimmer on my skull was very painful. Brother Izydor, who cut my tonsure out with a razor, wasn't too precise. It looked more like a hexagon than a circle. It was still twenty minutes to the end of the recreation period, so I went to the chapel to calm down. In the darkness, by the barely fluttering light of the eternal lamp, I felt better.

Wednesday, May 14

In my notebook I mark down the thoughts that flow through my head like spring clouds: some are long and complicated, I am unable to straighten them out; others are shallow and barely touch the subject that I am poring over like a blacksmith over a white-hot horseshoe. I would prefer to be free and independent, to look around my interior, because God, or my imagination decorate it and light it up differently every day.

When light escapes from my soul, I hear the voices of Brothers quarreling on the other side of the wall. I begin to struggle with the devil anew, who really is nothing. He stumbles all over the monastery just to sow confusion.

Friday, May 16

It happens to me more often that I fall into a reverie. One stubborn thought absorbs my entire attention. Although I attend different classes, ranging from meditation and Mass in the morning, participate in the Way of the Cross, recite the breviary, stroll up and down the hallways or garden, that same topic continues to bore into my head. I can't even describe it. During meditation in the chapel I pass my eyes over the walls, catch an imaginary fly or mosquito in my hand. As if I were unable to control my imaginings, which normally arrange themselves in some sort of logical array and give us the satisfaction that we are not animals driven by blind impulse.

Lately all abstractions, insights of my tired brain I let loose, let them wander wherever they like, so long as they don't associate themselves with my headache.

Anchorites out in the desert must have had similar feelings. They did not know psychologists who could explain to them what is real and what a mirage happens to be drawing for them in the air. Their skulls smoked like boiler rooms, they tried to overcome the resistance of matter, they broke time barriers, all the seasons of the year melted into one. They were not interested in Fridays, Sundays or Wednesdays in the church calendar. They slept during the day, kept vigil at night under the compass of glittering stars. Their tongues hardened in their throats like roots sticking out from the soil. Neither people not God knew when they actually departed from this world.

Sunday, May 18

I read in the "Legend" that Abbott Agathon used to place a stone in his mouth for three years before he learned how to be silent. The motivation for this behavior could have been the belief that speech distracts. It dissociates threads of thought that had been sorted out during meditation. Another person may turn out to be a nightmare, he may be redolent of frustration, and his skin may peel like on an antelope. He might have eaten meat with gravy on Friday; he might not have washed his ears or his genitals for a whole month. He has sand in his hair, dirty knees and his armpits stink.

Abbott Agathon by keep keeping his tongue in check saved his body a lot of energy essential for continuous prayer. He used to say to his disciples: In every other kind of work man has some kind of rest, then one, however, who prays, is engaged in a hard battle, labors in the sweat of his brow.

May 22

Dear Mother,

We took a long walk today. The May wind out in the field was violently pushing itself in under our tunics; it tugged at our hoods and scapulars. I had pleasure watching how the skinny Novice Master performed an amusing balancing act walking along a narrow strip of grass along two small fields of rye. I very much needed this escape out into open space from the narrow hallways and stonewall.

I have probably already written you that for some time I have had persistent headaches. I have the feeling that some kind of horrid bug is making itself a nest above my right ear under my skull. Pain, which is hard to bear, appears at the most unexpected moments. It disappears for a moment, only to return with even greater fury. I had already mentioned this to the Novice Master, but just in passing and I am not sure that he took it seriously. I feel helpless, I do not know if I should bother others with these kinds of matters.

When you come to see me I will give you two notebooks of my notes. I will feel more at ease if they are under your care. In moments when you will be alone, maybe you will get the urge to find out what is really going on in my head.

Please greet Krystyna, Irena and Janek cordially for me. Please ask them to remember me – in their prayers. Have you had any correspondence from Sister Florencja? She appears and disappears in my thoughts like a butterfly. Maybe she is having troubles that she is not informing us of?

With filial devotion, your helpless
Modest-Marcin

Monday, May 26

Reading the Old Testament is a great adventure, beginning with Moses' Pentateuch, the historical books and the books of wisdom. I never had the courage to plunge into this "vastness of the ocean" I did not have the time nor the preparation for it. Now I have time, though I continue to feel inadequately initiated. I read haphazardly, today Jonah appeared from the vastness of the waters, one of the twelve minor prophets.

Yahweh recommends that Jonah go to Nineveh and announce to its sinful residents that soon lightning and condemnation will strike the city. Jonah, like a true Jew, begins bargaining with God. He is quite sure what it is that God is trying to get him into. Sensing however that bargaining with God won't lead him anywhere, he wants to deceive Him. He gets on a ship in Jaffa, which is going West to Tarsus, and not in the direction of Nineveh.

An angry Yahweh unleashes a violent storm at sea. A hurricane and agitated waves toss the ship about like a nutshell. The crew keeps bailing water from the ship day and night. Everybody is fatigued beyond measure. Meanwhile one of the passengers is sleeping peacefully below deck, as if nothing were happening. One of the discontented sailors notices this and begins a quarrel. Others, stricken with fear, try to find a scapegoat.

Jonah smells a rat, he knows that the trick Yahweh wanted to play on him, won't work. He surmises that the huge roiling of the waters on the ocean is a sign of God's anger. Jonah admits to the sailors that he is a Hebrew and worships God, who created the sky, the ocean and the land and that in defiance he decided not to surrender to His will.

"Take me and throw me into the sea," he says with resignation, "and the waters will stop rising up against you."

The sailors gladly accept the proposal to get rid of the burdensome passenger. Jonah, heaved over the side, sinks to the bottom like a stone. At that critical moment Yahweh order the whale to swim up and swallow the drowning man. Jonah spends three days and three nights in the monster's stomach. In the insides of the whale, like in a temple, he prays to his God, pleading for survival and forgiveness.

When the whale finally spits the prophet out onto the beach, the latter submissively takes off for Nineveh and from morning to night announces to the residents Yahweh's words:

"Just forty more days and Nineveh shall be destroyed."

The warnings reach the king of Assyria. Nineveh repents and Yahweh shows compassion to the city, setting aside the death sentence.

Jonah's hitherto dormant ambitions boil up. The proclaimed threat of the pogrom vanished like smoke and sailed off with the wind. It seemed to him that in the eyes of the crowd he looked like a liar, his bombastic predictions were not fulfilled. Full of wounded bitterness, he turns to God:

"Now Yahweh, please take my soul away from me, for it is better for me to die than to live.

Wednesday, May 28

I can't stop thinking of Jonah's adventure with God. If I were a psychologist I'd probably have an easier time understanding their behavior. It is apparent from the narrative that God's intentions regarding the Ninehvites brought on the conflict in the private life of the prophet, which had to be resolved somehow. But neither God nor Jonah wanted to give up their case and their habits. In running away, Jonah tries to wiggle out of the mission Yahweh has in mind for him, like an eel. God has plenty of wonders up His sleeve, so he arranges for Jonah to sleep for three days on the belly of the whale. Submerged in darkness, enveloped by the gastric stench, Jonah quickly wises up. He has to wise up.

God saves Nineveh after Jonah's completed mission, but he submits him to a test for the second time. Jonah's personal ambitions became a laughing stock, in the eyes of the Ninehvites he looks as if he had been telling them tall tales, as if he wanted to intimidate and ridicule them. His personal rancor is so deep that Jonah would prefer not to be alive. He asks God to tear his soul out. Despite the disparities in the behavior of both partners, an outsider can draw an instructive conclusion.

God has no desire to destroy that in us, which we are. He plays rough with us only to the extent of the strengths that lie dormant in each of us. In the end He will gather all of us to Himself, but He wants to participate in the adventures of the individual creatures. A stone is just as dear to Him as fragments of light scattered all over the world. He drops silk cords down from the clouds for us that we can grab onto at any moment.

Saturday, May 31

One spot on the wall intrigued me during morning meditation. On the other side of the stained glass window the sun was sliding down from the roof onto the wall, sketching playful figures on the sidewall and on part of the ceiling. First I noticed the wing of an angel, a long arm, twisted curls of hair and his neck. At first I associated the sighting with a girl, but the figure rapidly took on the characteristics of a fiery cherubim. For a moment it entered my head that maybe this was a vision. The angel became more and more alive, lights and colors vibrated in him.

I called to mind the descriptions of visions that various saints had. I got carried away with feelings of piety, tears of joy filled my eyes. The apparition moved ever more quickly off the wall in my direction. It must have made a strong impression on me, because Brother Melchior who was sitting next to me whispered in my ear"

"Modest, meditate a little more quietly."

I couldn't understand what he was talking about. Meditation, after all, is done in silence, and our thoughts are not whirring spindles. After several minutes, however, the image began to be distorted, and a fallen angel emerged from the cherubim. Horns surfaced from the lock of hair, the cheeks, as beautiful as a girl's became covered with the skin of a toad. The colors were rapidly dying, and a thick blackness, like ink spilled out of an inkpot, pulsated on the wall in the sun. I began rubbing my eyes in disgust.

After all, such hallucinations shouldn't appear on a wall in a chapel in the presence of the Blessed Sacrament. I was afraid to move my head, so that the frightened eyes of the brothers and priests wouldn't deepen my dread even more. I don't know how long all that could have lasted. The fact is, that when the brothers began reciting the breviary, I was totally unprepared. I did not know which part of the prayer I was to start from, and on what page it was.

I furtively glanced across Brother Sebastian's arm, to fall into the correct recitation rhythm. But I was unable to get rid of the image for a long time, which, as if tattooed there, stuck under my eyelids.

Tuesday, June 3

I could not comprehend this: Satan was wreaking unbelievable temptations in the monastery! Everything that I am looking at here symbolizes the presence of God. In the tabernacle Christ is concealed in the Eucharist. The eyes of Our Lady of Częstochowa are looking at me from the altar. In the hallways the hermit saints follow out every step. There are also the sensitive eyes of the Novice Master, the Prior and the Confessor, registered in detail every grimace of surprise or anxiety on our faces.

Despite this I feel that the Devil is finding ways to instill dark duality in my mind, emptiness that irritates the heart and experiences of the flesh heated up by the senses. Time honored rules are incapable of controlling all thoughts and desires, even when I pull the wool hood over my head and hide in its shadow.

Thursday, June 5

Early in the morning the Novice Master and the Prior left for Jasna Góra. It was decided that Father Roman would take us for a walk "to the rocks," on the road to Janów and Złoty Potok. We were all excited. It was hot this week, the kitchen odors penetrated the cells and into the hallways. Each one of us also added his personal "odor sanctitatis" to the specific smell that spreads around the monastery.

After dinner, in the span of barely several minutes, everybody was ready to go. Brothers Arsenius and Bogumił as usual rushed to the head of the pack, and the others without haste, but with the distinct need to get outside, tried to keep up with them. Although the heat had not let up, a delicate breeze out in the open brought the anticipated relief.

On exiting the monastery I came across Brother Nepomucen. Thus far we didn't have the chance to hold a longer conversation. Three years older than me, already a high school graduate, he regarded us with a slight wink of the eye. His remarks during discussions seemed more sensible than ours. His left eyebrow had a strong slant. This gave the impression that he wanted to force his way into everybody's insides with his left eye. During walks he sweated easily, he would wipe his neck and temples with a handkerchief every few moments. He rolled the sleeves of his robe almost up to his elbows, pulled the front part of his scapular over on the left side. I looked in his direction as if I were waiting for an explanation:

"Why carry so much cloth on one's back? We should go for walks in sneakers and sports clothes."

At first I didn't know how to react, but I replied:

"The robe is some form of penance. Also the outer garb of the monk."

"Penance is the slowing down of natural development. Man like a mouse has to sleep enough, eat, and run a bit, to develop naturally. I spent seven months with the Pallotine monks. Their way of life is different. I decided to look for a more severe Order, it seemed to me that they were a bit too secular. Now I have to give them a lot of credit."

"I don't know much about the Pallotines," I muttered, "In Częstochowa on Kordecki Street they had the Divine Mercy chapel. I sometimes went to their chapel, the atmosphere inside was friendly and I liked to light a small candle there and say a prayer."

From that moment on the conversation moved along at a livelier clip, but we had to speed up our march, because the two "trotters" were way ahead of us. A kilometer from the rocks a rain cloud appeared in the sky, a wind sprang up and it began raining cats and dogs. There was nowhere to hide. Nothing but fields all around, rye or barley, here and there along the unplowed strips between fields grew juniper bushes. After several minutes our robes, pants and shirts were drenched. Mother Nature doubled the several kilograms of weight - our clothes. Everybody became crestfallen; nobody was prepared for such an adventure.

Father Roman deserved the most sympathy. Soaked through like the rest of us, constrained by the robe that was clinging to his skin, he presented a pitiable picture. Furrows appeared on his gaunt face, his large brown eyes looked like little dishes full of ants running in all directions. He was walking in the company of Brothers Melchior and Bosco. The latter, a head taller, waved his hands around, encouraging us to hurry up. It was closer and closer to the rocks. The sudden rain seemed to have exhausted its possibilities. The sun appeared on the at the edge of the hills that we were heading toward and like a cosmic rocket it was heading in our direction.

Due to the softened ground we needed a full quarter hour to reach our destination. Father Roman allowed us to take off our hoods and scapulars, but not our tunics. We hung them on tree branches and juniper bushes. After a couple of minutes everything was white, green, and a little weird. The navy blue cloud, like a deflated balloon, moved off to the East. The sun started to warm things up again, and steam, visible with the naked eye, rose from the fields. Everybody started wagging their tongues again, and it became quite noisy.

There were problems on the way back. Several brothers, together with Father Roman, had woolen robes.

Water doesn't evaporate from them easily. Others, including me, had robes made of substitute material, probably cotton or polyester. The water had partly evaporated from the hoods and scapulars that were hung on the branches. Some of the brothers stepped aside to more secluded spots, took off their pants and wrung the water out of them.

The greatest discomfort, which took its toll on everyone, was the inability to dry out the underwear, the shorts and T-shirts. For the first time I was able to observe collective irritation, a lack of logic in the strict adherence to regulations. I suppose that in every other instance, on scouting trips, the command to dry one's underwear would have been purposeful and appropriate. There would have been jokes of course, mutual peeking and derisive comments. Nonetheless, for a group of people condemned to constantly be together, that would not have had any greater significance.

The return to the monastery in wet robes was difficult and burdensome. Two or three daredevils took off their wet pants and wrapped them around their waist under the scapular or on their back under their hood. That gave them a small hump and gave rise to mocking remarks by their colleagues. The bravest ones tried to conquer the distance in full gear, that is, in a wet robe, wet underwear and pants. We walked to a much slower tempo. Nobody was in a hurry anymore. Even brothers Nepomucen and Bogumił found themselves in the middle of the double file.

Half way home many realized that the wet clothes rubbing against the skin was causing friction and irritation. Everybody was dragging their feet a little bit differently, depending on the places where the irritations occurred. Brother Melchior, ordinarily very humble, bowed out his knees like an old cowboy, and Brother Pafnucy was constantly adjusting something in his crotch and holding his tunic up in the air like a ballerina. We returned to the monastery with a huge delay, very tired. During supper the food disappeared quickly from the serving dishes. That got the brother cook worried, because he was scraping the rest of the buckwheat groats from the bottom of the pot and pouring the last pitcher of yogurt into the serving bowl.

Sunday, June 8
Spending time outdoors usually regenerates my strength. Sunday is difficult. Two Masses, sermons, the transits from room to room, lack of open space and air. I have the feeling that in comparison to others I am lagging behind. Good God, I am constantly preoccupied with how to avoid headaches, internal numbness, and not with how to contemplate more, see, experience, feel and do something for my neighbor. How small are my accomplishments in comparison with anybody else. My ship isn't sailing to anywhere anymore, it is filling up with water.

Monday, June 9
It is already June. My friends in Henryk Sienkiewicz High School are preparing for their final exams. At the

end of the month they will be promoted to the eleventh grade. I will be one year behind them. I wonder what I could have achieved that would have been better during the ten months of my stay in the novitiate. I probably increased the scope of my spiritual goods. I am probably a better person. I see sins and transgressions in me that I would not have noticed before. My knowledge of hermits is greater, I feel closer to the Egyptian anchorites than I do to my former school buddies. I gave up sports entirely, I don't play volleyball, basketball, and I don't kick a soccer ball around. A robe hangs between my knees. A once dormant body now bothers me more insistently. My dreams about girls are now more colorful and sensual, than they had ever been before. I am haunted by dreams four times more frequently, they all fuel expectations that will never be fulfilled.

My relationship to my family has changed a lot, my mother has grown like a church tower, she reaches the clouds, and my father has become authoritative. In my thoughts I search for some of his sayings, which I wasn't listening to before. He has become more logical than when I was with him every day. I often think about my brother, it seems to me that he is lonely. He misses my friends. We always were rivals on the sports field. We counted goals kicked into the net like valuable pre-war coins. Blood ties are no doubt stronger than monastic ghosts, than air that one breathes in common, than the basin in which everybody washes their faces and feet.

I wonder if the headaches would have been tormenting me had I not joined the novitiate. I had never before exploited my mind with such intensity. Sports and muscle feats were in the foreground. Now I want to explore the mysteries of my soul, completely neglecting my body. I look for angels around me. I want to feel the brush of their wings on my own skin. During meditation I stimulate my expectations, which the winds carry like leaves, further and further. And I keep waiting for the light of enlightenment to go on in my head and for the Holy Spirit to enter my heart.

Friday, June 13

There must have been another sharp attack against the Church in the press, because the Novice Master began talking about the prophecies of St. Malachi and about the difficult times which are to come for the popes. The end of our century is to become a time of brutal warfare between good and evil. It turned out that Brother Longinus knew quite a lot about this subject. He even had a brochure about St. Malachi, and in it a list of nicknames (over one hundred) that one can attribute to the reigning popes.

Suddenly we all became interested in the prophecies that the Irish monk, and later the Church dignitary who was an ordained bishop and archbishop, had written down in the twelfth century. The very serious and sympathetic attitude of the Novice Master toward these prophecies encouraged us to study them. Pope Celestine II (died in 1143) begins the list of popes and the pope with the number one hundred eleven ends it. The last pope is to be

Piotr II, a Roman. His motto will be Gloria Olivae (Glory to the Olive Tree). He will be the head of the Universal Church in the days immediately preceding the end of the world. When he reaches the end of his reign, the city on the seven hills, that is, Rome, will be destroyed. Then also Christ as the Judge will begin to judge all the nations and every person individually. These prophecies end more or less in the year 2010.

I must admit that many of us were plunged in fear and sadness. How is it possible that humanity will last for only half a century more and we will die at barely 65 years of age? So why the mental effort then? Why gather all these spiritual assets, why struggle with suffering, why look backward or forward? It is best to wait for the cataclysm, the second coming of Christ in a safe harbor like a monastery. And our wanting to do something good and it turning out bad won't justify us before the Judge coming to separate the wheat from the chaff.

June 14

My dear, good Mother,

I regret a bit that I have lost this school year. I feel a void, because I am not sure what it is in reality that I have learned in the novitiate. My spirituality is still shallow, naïve, without a proper perspective. You have to be open in matters of religion. Absolute honesty is a measure of spiritual progress. And my imagination, like the head of a rag doll, is more concerned with colorful paper hair curlers, the impression that my hands folded in prayer make on others, than with the living God and my neighbor. I feel that I will not save myself by imagination alone. It is a product of the brain, of my good or bad mood. And the world around me, which I can touch with my sight, squeeze in a clod of earth, is so beautiful and enormous. I could walk straight ahead my whole life and not see its end.

I am glad when on Tuesdays and Thursdays we go out for walks, I love open space, my body breathes easier. Fields divided by unplowed strips of grass arrange themselves into a black and green chessboard. Merry birds whirl about in the air like scattered handkerchiefs. Here and there ants hurry along – to their underground chapels, for vespers. It seems that space, filtered through the breath of angels, envelopes the world ever more tightly.

Mom, please give a warm hello to Dad and Janek for me, and congratulate him on his good grades and finishing the school year. We are now separated by only one year. After this year long laziness, staying away from textbooks and school, the desire to return to study is swelling in me. I hope that I will now notice more details in the textbooks than I had noticed ever before. In the monastery you have to ally yourself with study, otherwise boredom kills natural quickness of mind in us and stifles the desire to get to know the world in detail.

Lovingly,
Your son

Monday, June 16
Today I went to Żarki to see a neurologist with Father Roman, the Novice Master's assistant. He wanted

me to tell him in detail, in my own words, when the pain comes, how long it stays and what medication I take for relief. I had the impression that he understood these kinds of illnesses. He directed us to the municipal hospital for an X-ray. The next visit is in two weeks, when the X-ray negatives come back from the hospital.

The doctor did not speak with me, but with Father Roman, so I couldn't tell exactly what type of disease this is. I think they were talking about benign and malignant tumors. Father Roman did not have a particularly frightened look, so I could deduce that the disease would go away in due time just like it came. The doctor finally recommended cold head compresses and cold showers. That is supposed to help loosen up my inner tension. There should be no problem with the compresses, I will wet a towel in the sink and that's all. I suspect the matter of the shower will be more complicated. There is one bathtub in the entire monastery and as a novice I have the least right to it. The Novice Master also recommends that we bathe in our long nightshirts so we don't give ourselves the opportunity to see our naked bodies. Looking at a naked body, even one's own, may open us to indecent temptations.

We came back from Żarki by municipal bus. We barely made it for evening contemplation. Both visits took almost the entire day. That evening I was unable to concentrate on anything much. The headache would come suddenly – like an unwanted guest. I did get a prescription for a painkiller, but the pharmacy won't have it ready until tomorrow. I had to fend for myself somehow. I had already consumed all the "Little Roosters" from the novitiate pharmacy. All that was available was aspirin.

Dear Krystyna,

What remains to the end of the novitiate is half of June, all of July and three weeks of August. The shore is already visible from our boat. A week ago one passenger left us, Brother Nepomucen, whom I felt close to. He was older than the rest of us, knew more about life, often pouted at the Novice Master's recommendations, it seemed that he knew more. He has probably already reached his family in Nowa Wieś near Wrocław. This loss made an impression on all of us. When he was leaving his tonsure had not yet grown back on his head, his hair had not grown back even by two centimeters. He vanished like an icicle turned to water. Some of the brothers learned of the whole event only two days later. The Novice Master did not make any use of this subject. As if he himself were ashamed that suddenly his front tooth had been pulled out and he won't have anything to collect the tidbit off the fork with.

Earlier this week I went to the doctor. Mother probably told you about this. The headaches became really annoying and despite my good intentions to tolerate all hardships that life might bring, I had to surrender. I am waiting for the x-ray and a more detailed diagnosis. For now I am feeding on the fear that something more horrible may happen to me. Up to now I have been gorging on medication from our novitiate pharmacy, but they are no longer enough. I slept better the last two nights; the drugs prescribed by the doctor helped me.

Now I worry that, having made it halfway through the novitiate, I am beginning to fall apart and I won't have enough strength to make it to the finish line. I don't know if a handicapped creature like me at present, can be laid on the altar for God... After taking the vows I will officially become a monk. I can continue my studies up to graduation, get to know philosophers and theologians better, the history and dogma of the Church, and with the tonsure on my head, a symbol of temperance, I can be ordained a deacon or a priest.

At the very thought that I can accomplish all this in my life, I feel joy and astonishment. But after a minute, the happiness evaporates, and the amazement quickly turns into horror and trembling. More than ever I know long for conversations of the kind that we used to carry on between us, and to the domestic mood uncontrolled by time.

With a request for prayer
a frightened – Modest
and a scared – Marcin

Monday June 23

Apparently a storm was coming, because it was muggy and stuffy since early in the morning. Luckily it was Monday, and not Tuesday or Thursday, days when we normally go out for walks. In the afternoon, during our weekly "culpa," the public profession of our minor transgressions, a storm did pass over the monastery. After several loud thunderclaps, and a sudden downpour, the wind blew away the humid air and one could breathe normally again.

We also witnessed some unscheduled fun. After a short prayer we began, as usual, to walk up to the altar and in the presence of the Novice Master, profess aloud our minor transgressions of the regulations. Brother Fabian, who often doesn't choose his words too well, accused himself of "making noise with his seat during meditation in the chapel." Everybody burst out laughing, even though we knew that his bench creaks on sitting down and getting up.

Brother Sylvan confessed that he was cleaning a spot on his robe with his toothbrush. Brother Bosco as always reproached himself for talking too much and sometimes "gets stuck on long syllables." Brother Elias pounded a nail into the wall with the heel of his shoe and "beat up the wall pretty bad." It was my turn, and I didn't quite know what to say. On the way to the altar I remembered my spider, so I said that I often feed a spider with flies and centipedes. The Novice Master could ask additional questions, give a reprimand or assign penance. One had to wait patiently until he knocked on the bench. At times it was a long wait. This time he said: "As penance you will, brother, clean all the cobwebs in the refectory and the hallways." Somewhat taken aback, I marched back to my bench, which, surprisingly, also gave a loud creak.

Wednesday, June 25

An incredible thing happened tonight after midnight. Strange noises woke me up, a loud swallowing of air, laughter or crying – at first I couldn't tell which. After a while I realized that in the left corner, by the window, Brother Pafnucy was restlessly tossing on his bed. I held my breath. It seemed that he was struggling with himself, whispering something, as if he were speaking to someone. Suddenly his metal bed started to creak, vibrate and then again stretch its springs.

Brother Pafnucy was very close to me, I followed his example, and he amazed me with his modesty and humility. Sometimes he amazed everybody. I began to pray for him, guessing that he was probably struggling with impure temptation. After a minute he jumped up from his bed, dug around with his hand in his shaving kit and ran out into the hallway. Moonlight was feebly illuminating the cell. Brother Fabian's lusty snoring woke me up entirely. In the half-darkness I noticed his hairy left calf and heel sticking out from under the quilt.

I fought the desire to close my eyes again. The seconds and minutes kept ticking away, but I wanted to wait until Brother Pafnucy returned. At a certain moment I decided to take a walk to the bathroom. I was a little scared, lest it look like a romantic get together in the bathroom. Curiosity, or maybe the desire to help my fellow man, was nonetheless stronger than my fearful forebodings, that a third person might suddenly appear. Quietly, in socks worn out at the heels, I approached the bathroom. When I opened the door slightly I felt a soft breeze. The window to the outside must have been ajar. I slipped inside almost imperceptibly. Water was trickling with a hiss from the incompletely turned off faucet.

What I saw surpassed my wildest expectations. Blood was spilling out onto the floor. Brother Pafnucy, curled up tightly, was clutching his underbelly. A huge red spot was rapidly growing on his nightshirt. I grabbed my head. The pale, terrified face of Brother Pafnucy raised itself imploringly in my direction. A bloody razor lay on the floor by the sink. The same one he used every day to scrape off his thick growth. Pafnucy looked at me and whispered:

"I cut my genitals. Modest, help me!"

There was no first aid box in the bathroom. Nothing but toilet paper. I rocketed back to the cell, grabbed a part of my robes in the darkness and ran back. With the razor that I picked off the floor I blindly sliced the cloth into pieces and handed them to Brother Pafnucy, so he could bandage his wound. All the pieces were quickly soaked with blood. Terrified, we started mumbling something to each other. I insisted that the Novice Master be informed at once. At first Pafnucy protested, but fear and his weakened condition due to the blood loss did their job and he stopped protesting. I had to quickly dress in at least my tunic, to run one flight down and call for help. I banged on the door nervously and yelled loudly:

"Brother Pafnucy cut himself, he's bleeding a lot!"

The Novice Master laid his long, skinny finger on his lips.

"Quieter," he whispered, " it's night and everybody's asleep. Where is Brother Pafnucy?"

"In the bathroom!"

"In the bathroom? Let's go, quick..."

I ran ahead, taking two steps at a time, and he was right behind me. Brother Pafnucy, white as a sheet of paper, was leaning against the wall. Blood-soaked scraps of robe were strewn all over the floor. The terrified Novice Master looked all around and in a wheezing whisper ordered me to run to the Prior, and have him immediately call the ambulance. As I ran down the hallway I glanced at the clock; it was only 2:20 a.m.

The Prior, disturbed by me, was in no hurry to call for the ambulance. He said he wanted to see for himself what happened, and he ordered me to lead him to the site of the accident. He and the Novice Master conferred for a long time. Then he went down to the gate, to the main telephone. The Novice Master told me to take Brother Pafnucy under the arm. We started walking down to the floor below to the exit.

Meanwhile Pahfnotsy was clearly losing strength. By the exit, in the hallway, the light was on, the door was open. The Prior was walking back and forth outside. From time to time he observed the main entrance to the monastery in the beam of his flashlight. He was clearly upset. I surmised that in the hospital he would have a hard time explaining what happened. Maybe tomorrow or the day after somebody will try to make fun of this incident in the press. In a secular state monasteries and monks are treated as a necessary evil, dinosaurs from a by-gone era.

The ambulance came after twenty minutes, disturbing the quiet of the night with its moaning siren. Pafnucy was laid on a stretcher, which was slid into the ambulance. The Novice Master got in too and drove off to the hospital together with the wounded brother. He instructed me to find a piece of rag and wash off the blood spots in the hallway and the bathroom. He also made it clear that I shouldn't have any conversations with the other brothers on this subject. Not trying to wake anybody else up anymore, I wiped away the stains with the wet remainder of my white scapular. I wasn't sure whether I hadn't omitted some blood in the hallway. I could have overlooked something in the dim light.

Crawling back into my cooled-off bed, I thought about this incident as if it were a dream, of the kind that sometimes appear in the head in such realistic detail that it's hard to distinguish them from reality. This time I really wanted what had happened to have been just a dream. I hoped that when I woke up in the morning, life would again return to its well-worn routine. Before I fell asleep I realized that I had cut my scapular up into pieces and that in two hours, when I will be getting up to go to chapel for contemplation, I will not be completely dressed. I was still shaking inside.

Friday, June 30
A visit at Dr. Podleski's. The doctor is looking at

an x-ray photo on a matt, back-lighted glass pane on which the inside of my head is clearly visible. He shows and explains to Father Roman what he is able to read from the plate. There is, indeed, a spot on the plate the size of a walnut. I would prefer to be part of this discussion. After all, this is about my head and my health.

After a while the doctor asks me to strip down to the waist. I take off my robe and my T-shirt. The doctor looks into my eyes and my throat, and examines the glands in my armpits with his fingers. He says that a tumor is growing inside my skull above my right ear. It is not clear what shape it will take and if it is malignant. It might be a cancerous growth that attacks the auditory nerve or it could be a polyp that can be removed surgically. It'll require one more trip to the hospital for a sample of the tumor for microscope analysis. I am to report to the hospital again on Monday, that is, on July 7th.

Wednesday, July 2

I am worried by the thought that Satan can cause physical damage to a person, and take control of his body! That is totally uneven combat, in which the spirits have the advantage over us. They can dig in our thoughts like a hen on the farmyard garbage heap. They peck out every seedling of good inspiration. To tempt us successfully they have to outpace our thoughts by a split second. These struggles from dawn to dusk are really wearing me out. I wonder how I can escape from the tempter with my thoughts, how can I cover myself over with sand on the bottom, like a crab.

The spiritual guide constantly reminds us that we are here to multiply the good in us. The monk, like a bee in a hive, has to produce drops of honey every day. He has to earn his food, the roof over his head, decent shoes and the cloth from which the robe is sewn. All the contemplative monasteries in the Church thus explain the sense of their spiritual bustle. They have to produce values which are not, admittedly, the subject of interest of most people producing material goods, but which maintain a moral balance in the world.

It would be best if it were possible, but the power of the spirit, to make wicker baskets, or trace new paths in the clouds for ducks. And even better, if goods produced in factories could be exchanged for spiritual values, for instance:

For three glass, hand-made vases somebody becomes brave,

For weaving a wool rug, somebody achieves wisdom,

For building a sand hill in the form of a woman's breast, somebody regains their innocence,

For digging a seven-yard deep hole, somebody achieves complete forgiveness for their sins.

Friday, July 4

Something is happening to me. I feel as if the hot wind of summer were giving me more energy. Furtive thoughts like sparrows flutter about my ears every moment.

Everything that I look at all around me stimulates my brain to reaction. I have never before felt such inner animation. When I focus my attention, close my eyes, I feel the entire monastery building vibrating. I think I hear what the Brothers in the kitchen are doing. They're making a racket with the yet unwashed pots and plates, frying strip bacon on a pan to add to the cabbage, mixing split pea soup in a large aluminum pot, so it won't burn. In the Novice Mater's room Brother Rubin is repenting, digging petty transgressions out of his memory, which aren't worth a pound of donkey hair.

Yesterday, taking advantage of a similar mood, I was deliberating if it is possible to be outside one's body. I could wander up and down walls like a spider, change colors like a butterfly, adapt to coldness and coolness. No thoughts, not even feelings under the skin. Only a tiny fan, attached to my shoulder blades, which would allow me to move in space mile after mile.

I never supposed that such a kaleidoscope of thoughts could appear in a monk's head. If someone were to place a long strip of sheet metal against my temples now, it would no doubt start to ripple slightly, absorb the heat from my head. No doubt a candle placed on its surface would soften, and snow fluttering down from a cloud would melt on it.

Sunday, July 6

Brother Pafnucy returned from the hospital yesterday. Nobody knows anything concrete about his self-inflicted injury. I heard from Brother Fabian that "Pafnucy's appendix got busted and they took him to the hospital in an ambulance." The Novice Master neither confirmed nor denied this rumor. My keeping "my mouth shut" will probably improve the evaluation of my behavior. I was, as is evident, the only eyewitness.

Today after vespers we found ourselves alone together in our cell. Brother Pafnucy thanked me cordially for my help. He said he only needed six stitches and the wound should heal. During his hospital stay he was afraid that the superiors might not allow him to take his vows. The Novice Master spoke with the Father General and it looks like this time the offense will be forgiven. But they don't want any more "escapades" like this in the future. I was just about to tell him that tomorrow it was my turn to go to the hospital for a brain biopsy, but I restrained myself.

So far nobody knows my secret, the longer the better. The Almighty knows best why he burdened me with such a nightmare. I thought – a surgeon will also appear on my path, who will open my skull, sew my brain together with a few threads, tie the bones together with a few clamps and I'll be able to dream again, so I don't waste my youth.

Wednesday, July 9

I am still woozy from the anesthetic that they pumped into me while taking the sample of brain tissue from me. I didn't know that in these kinds of cases a hole is drilled in the skull and a special needle is then inserted that extracts a fragment for further analysis under a microscope. I was not discharged from the hospital after this "minor" operation, but had to remain under observation until the following day. I must have been incoherent, because I don't remember what happened after the operation.

That was my first night outside the monastery.

Thursday, July 10

The lives of the saints are my book of wisdom in the novitiate, as also the dialogues of the desert fathers and the frequent, and in fact daily lessons in asceticism by the Novice Master. Thanks to the general atmosphere that predominates here each one of us has an equal opportunity to become a saint, or at least learn elementary piety. I am writing about this without any contrariness. Sometimes I surrender myself with gusto to an avalanche of ascetic winds. Thanks to them I do not have to grapple with the pressure of my own thoughts, and the temptations of the evil spirit seem to become muted and to die down.

I am also experiencing a sort of euphoria with the spirits. The fancies on the subject of angels in my imagination have multiplied. I don't think exclusively about my Guardian Angel anymore, but also about angels that are all around like birds in the air and fish in water. I think of them in the plural, because I have become convinced that there are many of them, maybe even hundreds of thousands.

When Christ healed the possessed man of Gerasa he chased a whole legion of evil spirits out of him. They "entered swine, and the herd ran off a cliff into the sea and drowned." The conclusion is that a legion of angels is needed to stand up to a herd of devils.

If my imagination has carried me too far, the fault lies with the monastery, the walls and ceiling painted white, without any shades of color, the boring paintings, the naked pipes of the central heating system or those that carry water, hissing and buzzing like a snake laying an egg.

Friday, July 11
During the late morning conference the Novice Master told us how God deprived Friedrich Nietzsche of his reason several years before his death, because he had been proclaiming the philosophy of "the death of God'." In his book Human, All Too Human he maintained that the moral differentiation of good and evil was established by men who believed that certain actions are good for society, and others harmful. He also believed that conscience is shaped by parental authority, or the authority of our educators, and is not the voice of God.

According to the Novice Master "it wasn't possible to have thought up a more dangerous doctrine." It reminds of a story from the Old Testament about the tower of Babel, when the residents of Babylon thought that they could build "a city and a tower whose tip would reach the sky." The God of Israel didn't like this idea: Yahweh came down from heaven to take a look at the city and the tower and quickly came to the conclusion that "in the future nothing will be impossible for them, whatever they decide to do."

In his clairvoyant omnipotence He said: "Let us descend therefore and mix up their tongues, so that the one won't understand the other." The Novice Master explained that the constructors of the tower showed the same ambitions as the Tempter awoke in the first parents – they wanted to be equal to God, build a staircase that would lead to heaven. "There is nothing truer," the Novice Master tried to convince us, "than the inspired words of the Bible. God is our Comforter and expects love, loyalty and – faith from us. He cuts down all rebellion against Himself like weeds alongside a fence."

None of us in the novitiate would have been capable of such thoughts. Nonetheless Nietzsche's example made an impression on me. I knew from my readings that his father had died of a brain tumor, and his insanity was probably genetically conditioned. God did not have to punish him more. In my current state of health this example depressed me.

Monday, July 14
I shouldn't torment this notebook with my notes anymore. I rather do it to drown out the noises in my head,

some sort of fractured echo fragments, which make my life difficult to bear. Like in a resonating box I hear sounds, which are like throwing pebbles into bottles, or the irritating booming of a locomotive that has been knocked off its rails in an accident. The more I try to calm my interior; the worst is the squeaking of the cartilage in my head, the stretching and contraction of my tendons.

I don't know whom I should ascribe such clatter to, the Devil, God or maybe the illness, which arrived unasked and is destroying my organism. I usually break out in a cold sweat then that drenches my skin and armpits.

I now have to catch every word in my head, and when I get hold of it a moment later it crumbles in my mouth like sand. My most fervent prayers are like the sifting of grain in the field, from which the wind blows away the chaff and the dust. Despite this, I try to cross the footbridge over the abyss, find the stairs on the mountain slope which lead to the feathery clouds in which God the Father, my Creator and Savior, is hiding.

Thursday, July 17
An almost one and a half hour walk to the "hermitage." We were here before, but in the wintertime. Not much could be seen under the blanket of snow. The summer blanketed the forested elevation in green, with a big boulder sticking up in the middle like the club of Hercules. For our little, white-robed group this was an ideal place to stop. Small, huge and medium boulders stuck their bellies,

their crooked knees, their cemetery-stiff elbows, and their sand-encrusted heads out of the ground. There was plenty to sit on or rest one's back against. Several dozen knotty pines made themselves at home on the gentle slope, forming the embryo of a forest. Now and then a scared rabbit or a screeching jackdaw would jump out of a green bush. It was deserted and peaceful here, without any alien existences around.

To this day I do now know when we started calling this place "the hermitage." Wandering around in all directions each one of us was looking for a small adventure, which would get the attention of the others. Spontaneous outbursts of laughter cut the silence. Brother Fabian discovered an anthill nearby, under one of the pine trees. It was sizeable, maybe four and a half feet wide. The hard working ants were running everywhere around the pine tree. Brother Fabian, who liked to give long-winded discourses on every subject, was already trying to warn Brother Felix about the danger threatening him.

"Bro, if you want the ants to eat you alive, sit your ass down in the middle of that anthill!"

"I thought that only termites devour people," Brother Felix tried to defend himself.

"Are you kidding, termites only eat wood and wood rot, ants eat whatever their buzz- saw mandibles come upon. They swallow forest fruit, insects and the honey-sweet excrescence of aphids."

"How do you know this?"

"I'm from the countryside, from the forest, and

I know all about crickets and ants; better than you, Bro, know theology!"

"How many of those human-eating ants might there be here?"

"Probably several thousand, or maybe more. They no doubt have their tunnels under this mound, connected with walkways; birthing chambers in which the queen ant lays her eggs, and pantries where they store their provisions for the winter. They dig two or three yards down into the earth, so they don't freeze in the winter."

"I heard that they are very well organized, maybe even better than we are in the monastery?" Brother Melchior chimed in, having listened in on the discussion.

"You better believe it, Bro, that they're better! They have their queen, in other words their Prioress that a regiment of males beds every now and then so she can lay her eggs. When an egg transmutes into a larva, and the larva into a chrysalis, and an ant comes out of it, then the whole game begins all over again. Female ant workers and nurses take care of feeding, educating and preparing the young generation for the novitiate, while the queen ant, after laying many hundreds of eggs, relaxes and dreams of a new opportunity, when athletic and rested males again start forcing her to sin."

"Fabian, you have a very colorful imagination and an unbridled tongue," Brother Melchior chimed in again.

"Father Walerian's ears will swell when you tell him about this nonsense."

"Melchior, aren't you overdoing it a bit with that confession. We aren't talking about girls now, just about ants. And if every Prioress during her term of office gave birth to a few female novices for the convent, maybe that is not such a bad idea."

Fortunately the conversation broke off when the Novice Master reminded us that it was time to start heading back. The afternoon had zipped by. There was a long march ahead of us. Along the way, as usual, we will be saying the rosary.

Oh, late afternoon star, pray for us.

Monday, July 21

I familiarized myself with the biography of Sister Maria Faustyna, that is, of Helena Kowalska of the Congregation of Our Lady of Mercy. In my breviary I have a bookmarker with a picture of Jesus, painted according to her instructions, with white and red rays spurting from His heart. Brother Melchior mentioned to me several days ago, that he was very impressed by her "Little Diary." She wrote it at the express bidding of her confessors. After several weeks of living in the congregation she came down with tuberculosis. She was tormented by frequent returns of this disease until the end of her life.

As a nun under temporary vows she worked in various convents of the Congregation: in Warsaw, Vilna, Kiekrz near Poznań, in Płock, in Biała near Płock, in Warsaw and Cracow. On May 1, 1933 she took her perpetual vows. She concealed her diary writing from her fellow nuns; she placed a note in the preface for the curious: "No one is allowed to read the drafts and notes that are here... these are the recorded secrets of conscience..."

The Reverend M. Sopoćko, her Confessor, explains that because he was a professor in a seminary, he didn't have much time for long confessions. The wealth of Sister Faustyna's spiritual experiences and the graces bestowed on her were so enormous however, that the need arose to document them. The author of "The Little Diary" despite lack of a higher education, showed a lot of life wisdom and sound reason. Surrendered to the Will of God and full of enthusiasm, she spread the fame of the cult of Divine Mercy in whatever ways she possibly could.

Although I cannot compare my experiences even to the slightest degree with her revelations, nonetheless, even familiarity with the "Little Diary" gives me pleasure and encourages me to continue my notes. Also her example of fighting with illness is a great comfort to me at this moment. I repeat after her: Jesus, I Trust In You."

Wednesday, July 23
Oh so many things irritate me now, every petty sniping of my brothers. To boot, fate is knocking the tools out of my hands that I could have used to defend myself. My brain is starting to get lazy, and the will to endure does not know how to overcome blind, unreasoning matter. I feel like a garden snail crawling with the shell on its back from one brick wall to another.

I pray to God's Mercy for better health.

I repeat the litany to the Angels.

I am composing a poem in my head that I will probably never write.

I try to wrap a wet towel tightly around my head, before it explodes in a moment, punching holes in the ceiling and walls.

I try to be normal, although I know that it is probably no longer possible.

Sunday, July 27

I again allowed the Golden Legend to tempt me. Under the date of July 27 there's the story of the Seven Sleeping Brothers. It turns out that when the Emperor Decius ordered a temple erected in the middle of Ephesus, so that everyone would make sacrifices to the gods, many Christians became fearful. Severe punishments caused "friend to deny friend, father his son, and son his father." Seven brothers found themselves in a similar situation, which "were pained at what they saw all around them." So they decided to sell their inheritance, give it away to the poor and move off into the mountains, to lead a saintly life in concealment.

One day, "while they sat and conversed amid sad-

ness and tears, suddenly by the will of God they fell asleep."
Decius on being told that they had escaped him and were
hiding in the mountains ordered their cave entrance to
be plugged with stones. He supposed that they would die
there of hunger.

Many, many years passed before a citizen of Ephesus became interested in the mountain and ordered sta-
bles for his shepherds to be constructed in the plugged up
cave. Awakened by the sound of pick axes and shovels, the
saints jumped up, thinking that the emperor's messengers
had come for them. They were greatly surprised when they
found people who were friendly to them, who were interested in a better utilization of the cave, not in their arrest.
They sent the youngest among them to town to buy some
groceries and to get news about their relatives and family.

Meanwhile Ephesus was already a different city.
There was no trace of their friends and parents. And in
place of the oppressor Decius the God-fearing emperor
Theodosius was in power. News of the Seven Sleeping
Brothers spread like wild fire. The bishop of Ephesus,
moved by this incident, immediately went with the emper-
or and his retinue to the cave. At the sight of the Christian
emperor the faces of the saints lit up like suns. The bishop
said: "I am looking at you as if I were looking at the Lord
bringing Lazarus back to life!" One of them, St. Maximian,
replied: "We are truly resurrected and live, and as the child
in its mother's womb feels nothing from the outside, yet
lives, so we were alive, lying here, asleep and feeling nothing." After these words in plain sight of all those present

they bowed their heads to the earth and again gave up the spirit in accordance with God's intention. The bishop buried all the brothers one next to the other in the cave, "until the time when God resurrects them a second time," and the emperor commanded the place to be decorated with gilded stones." They slept the sleep of the righteous for one hundred ninety six years.

After reading the legend I had mixed feelings. In each biography I try to find a suitable example for myself. And here the winds bore me into a world that was rather unreal, dream-like and fabulous. How, after this reading, am I to distinguish "Sleeping Beauty" from "The Seven Sleeping Brothers?"

Maybe the dogma about the physical resurrection of our bodies isn't as difficult as we make it. It is sufficient to lift the anchor of our disbelief and set out onto the waters of the ocean regardless of the weather. Someday, years later, we will be able to make it back to shore.

Tuesday, July 29

Monk's Robes

When it lies, folded into a neat square, on the chair next to my bed in the cell, all sweaty under the arms, threadbare on the stomach and knees, it symbolizes my interior.

In the morning, so it won't feel alone, I fill it from the inside with my body, without disturbing any crease it's gotten used to; I also lend it my skinny neck and shoulders, so it can move vertically; I adjust my elbows and thumbs in the sleeves, so they can land where they want to;

in the evening during the Eucharistic procession in the basilica I lend it my feet, so it can parade with the faithful;

out of respect, so it won't get treated anonymously, I stick out my shaved head with its protruding ears, my nose, crooked after having bumped into a wall, and eyes with lowered eyelids.

We both must remember, we are symbols of a transcendental power, the luminescence of human transience, a sleep-inducing drug.

Apparently something got switched around in my head, because I wrote a poem instead of a regular note in my diary. I think it is just a paper brooch.

Monday, August 4
After dinner a walk in the garden. The sun was quite hot; there was not one puff of breeze. Maybe there are more wind gusts in the open fields outside the walls. I walked with Brother Felix, who stands out in our choir

with the pleasant tone of his voice. Brother Longinus sometimes quiets him down, when he tries to dominate. The domination of one voice does not always guarantee proper harmony of melody. His tenor, despite considerable power, is not angelically pure. The dregs left over from his recent change of voice have not yet been filtered out.

During the walk we returned to what we had been reading. The fantasized form of the biographies in the Golden Legend fascinated me, and Brother Felix enthusiastically talked about the Florentine Dominican monk Girolamo Savonarola. It turned out that it is difficult to classify that charismatic preacher. Some consider him to be a saint, an inspired prophet of his times; others, that he was an embodied anti-Christ; and others still that he was just a nervous man tormented by apocalyptic visions, which were the subjects of his sermons.

Brother Felix was excited by the way Savonarola hypnotized his audience from the pulpit. All of Florencja was at his feet. He threatened the rich, pointed out the bad habits of the clergy and the bishops. He even upbraided and scolded his own fellow monastic brothers. Brother Felix was of the opinion that such an enthusiasm for scolding the faithful could only be tolerated in a theocratic republic. In our country, a secular state that treats religion like an opiate befuddling the people, neither the faithful nor the church hierarchy would tolerate such acerbic slogans. Even though the good, like air, must bubble up from beneath the water to the surface.

Wednesday, August 6

My brain jumping like a frog being prodded with a red-hot rod causes me to see things differently than others. Especially since in the monastery every day is similar to the day that just passed and identical with the one that will come tomorrow and the day after tomorrow. The months are like weeks, and the year like the page of a week torn out of a calendar.

During meditation one can get carried off by one's imagination to the edge of time, when God created the world out of nothing, spun the first thread of light in the darkness, let stars that were too hot fall out of His hands, crushed the shells of planets that were not coherent enough; or else was amazed at Himself, as to why He had created the Devil, who was ruining many of His wise plans...

During contemplation one can die, looking as the shadows of trees outside the windows lengthen, as one's body cools, as the ears wilt, as the lungs throw out the rest of the carbon dioxide in them, as the brain cortex dries out like a cork.

Friday, August 8

During the evening recreation we discussed a difficult "theological" subject with Brother Longinus. The sun, red as a strawberry, was slowly getting ready to jump over to the other side of the planet. After a hot day the walk in the garden brought relief. After a few perfunctory sentences a question appeared in our conversation: is individual faith sufficient for salvation or is the collective faith of the Church sufficient?

I was aware that neither one of us was prepared for such a question. But like boys in shorts on a beach, we succumbed to the charm of the waves splashing onto the shore. Brother Longinus was of the opinion; someone somewhere had pounded this into his head, that participation in the monastic life itself is the basis for achieving salvation.

"We hopped onto a good train," he concluded, "and every one of us will make it to heaven. The train car wheels revolve when we recite the breviary together, participate in Mass, and go have something to eat in the refectory or recite the rosary during a long walk and look at the ravens out in the field. The trick is to not fall out of the train, not to allow another passenger to push us out a window. Our chief engineer is the Father General, and the Novice Master checks our tickets. You can't hitch a ride for such a long journey."

"It seems to me," I reacted, "that the belief that one can be collectively saved is just such a hitch-hiked ride. That's like somebody trying to reward or punish people for being men or women or only permitting whole classes to take final exams rather than individual persons."

Brother Longinus rolled up the sleeves of his robe somewhat, his short square hands were most obviously getting ready to rebut every argument that I might bring up at this moment.

"Just remember, brother, the celebrated discussion about the collective responsibility of the German nation for the crimes committed during World War II; or the discussions about French or Polish national vices; or even better the story, visible on every page of the Old Testament, that the Jews are a Chosen Nation."

The blow was strong. I tried to evade it.

"For me the collective is a strange, shapeless hailstorm cloud. The sun can't penetrate it, and singing swallows won't fly up to it."

"So you have missed your calling, brother. Individual characteristics are not of interest to the monastic collective. Heads all shaved pretty much the same, like military recruits, identical clothes, the cheapest shoes money can buy and everybody of the same height, down to the inch. Dwarfs with pimples deform the natural undulation of heads during a procession. For the same reason teenagers with long, skinny necks don't suit anybody's purpose."

I hadn't realized that he would toss his habit of directing a chorus into our discussion. I tried to extricate myself out of the situation.

"It seems to me that individual beauty and the attractiveness of specific individuals is the foundation for the varied richness of the community. I prefer fifteen varieties of roses and their many colors to a thousand weeds by the fence."

"You're a romantic, brother, the world happens to be spinning in the opposite direction."

We could have gone back and forth like that until the moon rose, but we had to go to the evening breviary liturgy. But nothing could knock me off the stream of reflections that we had initiated. I felt their flavor like red cherries on their branches.

Sunday, August 10

I looked through several pages of notes in my diary. I have to learn to write more simply. A larger scope is missing in these notes. Puttering around, walking from wall to wall down long, narrow corridors. Were it not for my memory and fragments of the flickering past, I would feel very lonely. How long can I live feeding myself on the rain of my own imagination?

Tuesday, August 12

I didn't sleep well at night and the knocking on my door aroused irritation in me. It seemed to me that it was only midnight. I raised my heavy head, filled with wet sand, from the pillow. I tried to gather enough energy to bring myself to order with a few splashes of water. But I felt that the wilted, sleepy body was holding back. I barely made it to contemplation.

The wooden bench was just as cozy as my pillow stuffed with chicken feathers. Instead of kneeling I sat down, pressing my back firmly against the back of the bench. A tiny flame of consciousness was barely glimmering in my head. Its light was slowly gaining strength. In my thoughts I sought a point of support, a subject around which I would be able to sort out the themes. Every fluffy cloud on the horizon could be a star that I was waiting for. But no eureka moment came.

It amazed me that physical sluggishness could cause such indolence of the mind. I wondered with what speed the blood of poets flows into their brains when they are writing poems, and with what speed it enters the brains of prophets when they try to enlighten the future with their vision. In my coarse-cloth hermit's tunic I am neither the one nor the other. At this moment I am incapable of either quicker movements or inspiring verses.

The wooden bench on which I am sitting is my throne. Shaped from imperfect clay, I dream of being showered with feathers from which stork wings would grow.

Friday, August 15

A subject that I can't free myself from – an intrusive "tenant" in my head bores me. It's because of him that I have no interest to see what's going on outside the window, to trace the rays of the sun, wait for drops of rain on the window pane. In chapel I lose my train of thought, and – the fervor that is needed in liturgical concentration. Not that long ago my thoughts were still obedient to me. I could extract them from a rousing bonfire in the field, from veils of smoke, and carry their pure flame before me.

I nourished my soul with a quote from a psalm or an Egyptian desert hermit's saying. I knew how to suck the juices out of every word, change an ordinary meditation into a prayer. Thought by itself, without ascetic fervor, behaves like a sluggish centipede – it seems to be climbing up the dusty walls, it wanders from one incline onto the next, ranging across the cracked ceiling in all directions, but when it feels exhausted, it falls like a dirty drop of water into a gray puddle, from which it was born.

August 16

Dear Irena,

Everything that was happening in the novitiate thus far was taking on good and foreseeable forms. It seemed to me that every day spent here multiplies the spiritual goods in my soul, that I am building and strengthening my character, eliminating vices, and in their place grafting virtues, and that in a short while, like Sister Faustyna, I will be able to draw on the walls with crayons the image of Christ which will appear in my reveries. My inner righteousness will protect my white robe from external threats. One day I will force my way through the barricades of the mystics and all their insider secrets with God, I will know how to imitate them and will make it to the sunny mountains of the saints and angels under my own power.

Meanwhile some sort of awful tumor in my head is devouring all the energies in me and is muddling my awareness. In the hubbub of constant fears I am losing my compass – of hope. And instead of joy at being in the Order and the quickly approaching celebration of taking my vows, I am tormented by fears of defeat, the collapse of all my life ambitions and common sense; the ruins of my emotional and physical health.

I don't want cruel fate to grind me down into the ground. I am rebelling like an animal being led to the slaughter. I am rebelling against my own body, which has let me down; against my family, from which I have inherited sick genes; against God, to whom I committed my life on the altar, figuring that he will take me from this world uncrippled and of sound mind. I am rebelling against the Order, to whom I gifted my insolence and courage, and also my barely awakened youth — which none of my superiors respected.

Now like a madman I am standing at the edge of the abyss. In the evening the sky, studded with stars, belches emptiness in my face, and during the day the sun hides behind a cloud of contaminated, poisonous gasses. Somebody is going to have to take responsibility for my disaster! And if nobody takes the responsibility, the fault will be mine anyhow. I was caught in the trap of helplessness of those who wanted to decide what to do with my life, etch virtues on my hide with a nail, which they themselves were incapable of practicing.

And yet I could have become a chimney sweep, a coal stoker loading coal into the furnace of a small ship, a wall paper hanger breathing in turpentine, a watchmaker repairing watches without their hands, or — a weight-lifter lifting weights. But I had the urge to fly higher, and was tempted by space like Icarus, by the desire to touch the divine Sun with my bare hands.

That is why today in the monastery, which should be a golden palace of all hopes, I am being corroded and destroyed from inside by despair, the mother of all madness.

Dear Irena, sorry for this complaint. I will never write you such a sad letter again, and please destroy this one after reading it.

Marcin

Saturday, August 16

A bat, fluttering its wings, flew over my head during my evening walk in the garden. I thought that it was some damned person's soul separated from its body. With both hands I instinctively grabbed my head, filled constantly with thoughts and feelings. It seemed weird to me however, that I associated an ordinary creature, woken up too early, with the soul of a damned person. The imagination of a monk probably isn't always guided by logic.

The evening air was brisk; dew started forming into droplets on leaves. I had no desire to return to the monastery, for monotonous prayer in the stuffy chapel. This was a clear violation in thought against monastic moral etiquette, against Jesus in the Tabernacle. It is scary to think that a couple of ounces of badly programmed cells in my brain make me so irritable and nervous. I would prefer to be myself, who I was up to now, even at the price of pounding wood splinters into my heels.

Sunday, August 17

During the afternoon recreation I was informed that my mother was waiting for me in the lounge. This was a pleasant surprise, such a meeting could only serve to improve my self-confidence, pull me out of the proverbial hole. Mother was very cordial. It had come to her attention that complications with my head could turn aside the friendly wind blowing into my sails. Everything was going smoothly at home. Janek made it into ninth grade without any problems and will be attending the Henryk Sienkiewicz's lyceum like I did.

Mother referred to her conversation with Father Eusebius, her confessor, that there should be no problems in allowing me to take my vows. She improved my mood with that news. I was amazed by her motherly thoughtfulness, loyalty and faith in my better future. For a moment I thought that I had mounted on a young tiger, and merciful God will return full functionality to all the cells in my brain. Providence had been watching over me thus far, why would it want to forego that now. I even wondered that I could be so deeply moved by my own happiness.

During the conversation the subject of the diary I am keeping came up. I realized that mother did not have a very good idea about it. I ran to my cell and brought her three notebooks. Every one of them contained notes from two or three months, practically from one quarter. Mother was astonished (me too) that there was already so much of it. She started feverishly flipping through the pages, reading fragments aloud haphazardly, taking out and putting back between the pages the letters that I had not mailed to their addressees. I saw how her enormous blue eyes were becoming more and more watery.

After her departure I went to my cell, to sort through the rest of my notes. I was left with a fourth notebook filled half way with my jottings. Despite my fatigue, I wrote a new note, so much had happened after all – I had successfully lived through yet another day.

Monday, August 18

A delicate knock on the door, during our spiritual reading, dislodged me from my reverie. It was Brother Ireneusz with instructions that I go see the Novice Master. On impulse my stomach jumped up into my throat. I wasn't sure what my superior might want form me, two days before the beginning of our retreat. Walking down the stairs I tried to guess the subjects that might be the reason for sending me home:

a) poor results in my spiritual life, a lack of higher aspirations,

b) my sick head, the rapid falling apart of my organism and my thoughts,

c) I am nothing, at most, a stalk drying up in the monastery garden.

The conversation at the Novice Master's desk, however, took a much milder course. On Monday September 1st, right after breakfast, I am to be all packed and ready to leave for Cracow. Together with Brother Joseph we will accompany the chauffeur in transporting clothes and other knick-knacks of the novice brothers to the monastery at Skałka. We will take the monastery's "Nyssa" van, which travels between the monasteries. The reason for my earlier departure is that Dr. Poleski had already contacted the Brothers Hospitallers Hospital in Cracow and was sending me for further, more detailed tests.

After leaving the Novice Master I was engulfed by a nightmarishly noisy joy. For it was already known that I was being permitted to take my vows, and that the tumor in my head maybe isn't all that horrible, since the physicians at the Brothers Hospitallers want to take care of it. Maybe the dangerous knocking in my head and the sudden pains are just my imagination. During the evening meditation I was happily floating under the ceiling of the monastery's chapel, like Bethlehem angels, I was turning cartwheels together with them. God had once again allowed himself a small, unselfish magnificence toward me.

> *Praise therefore my Lord, O my soul,*
> *And be glad in God, my spirit.*
> *Alleluia, Alleluia, Alleluia.*

Tuesday, August 19

As of tomorrow we begin a ten-day retreat. After a year-long marathon of struggles with our vices and bad habits, we are approaching the finish line. The Novice Mater will once again try to fashion us mortals, contaminated with original sin, into candidates for perfection.

We had the first foreshadowing of this in the remarks after Mass. It would be best if we observed strict silence during the period of the retreat. The talkativeness of monks always caused big losses in their inner life. Words spoken aloud cause nothing but chaos in thinking. We should now saturate our interiors with prayer, dialogue with God.

Man spends most of his time is isolation, even when he loses himself in a crowd on the street. Interior aloneness doesn't disgrace anybody; rather, it helps to multiply spiritual benefits. That is how the desert hermits acted, masters of the contemplative life, and we should act in a similar manner.

In our lives seconds are important. The sixty million seconds that make up the life of an average monk are barely a billionth of a second of the eternity in which God exists.

Thursday, August 21

Yesterday, a couple of minutes before going to bed, I had a very unpleasant experience. With my right eye, instead of seeing the light of the light bulb scattering on the ceiling, I noticed as if a rainbow of colors with a sizeable admixture of red. Since the left eye was seeing correctly, I squinted and observed both views. There was a distinct difference. After some time my upper eyelid began to twitch, I felt the skin above my eye contracting and wrinkling. I was very scared. The cold salamander of fear started prowling in my stomach again.

This was an alien experience for me, one I had never had before. Even when Brother Fabian shut the light off in the cell, my right eye was still having color flashbacks. I curled up inside like a cat that is ready to jump into a fire rather than get itself torn apart by the fangs of a hungry hyena.

For the next several minutes I was listening to what was going on in my body, what new maneuvers the parasite in my body was planning in my head. In the morning my right eye was very red, to all those who were interested I explained that I had poked myself in the eyeball with a pencil, in an absent-minded moment. But fear kept returning every now and then. I tested my vision by squinting now with my left eye, now with my right. The flashbacks kept appearing or blurring out, they combined or created ectoplasm in undetermined places.

August 23

Dear Son,

You probably began your retreat. I would like to calm you down in case your headaches should return. After a conversation with Father Markiewicz, the Definitor, I became convinced that the tumor you told me about is most probably connected with your adolescence. Hormones in a young body sow themselves like mushrooms after a rain, in the least expected places. Endure just this one more week, my love. They will test you thoroughly at the

Brothers Hospitallers Hospital in Cracow, maybe they won't even have to open your skull, to see what is going on inside. We will all be praying for the success of the procedure. Father Scholastyk, who is in Pinczów now, also had a similar incident. A gland the size of a pear made itself at home in his armpit. The operation was successful, now he is reputed to be the best preacher in the Order. The female students love him, even those studying Marxism.

I am reading pages of your diary together with Krystyna. We did not have a very good handle on a lot of matters. I am most delighted that you are reading a lot. Every newly read book is like a bottle of oxygen at the bedside of a patient.

With ardent concern and prayers for your health in front of the Miraculous Picture of Our Lady of Jasna Góra.

Mother

August 24

Dear Mother,

Thank you for your caring letter. The retreat is actually coming to an end. In three days we will be taking our eternal vows. The Novice Master now wants to make our insides whitehot. He wants us to act according to the rules of the spirit, and not flatter the body. "For the body," according to St. Paul, "nurtures cravings against the spirit, on the other hand the spirit desires something other than the body – they are so very opposite each other and therefore do what you don't want to do."

The battle between the spirit and the body takes place in

every person. In me too, except that my body is now jeering at all those lofty metaphors, at the heavens above the monastery, at all the saints and angels. That is why, day in and day out, I ask God for a miracle, for better blood circulation to my gray cells, so that my brain can finally start functioning normally again.

Despite all hope I pray that my life will turn for the better, when by the act of the triple vows, of obedience, purity and poverty, I will surrender my soul into the slavery of the angels and Our Blessed Virgin Mary.

Mother, my thoughts flow now like multiple eddies on a river, together with the leftovers of unfulfilled dreams, together with the croaking of frogs at the invisible jaws of an invisible enemy.

With words of faith, hope and attachment,
Your son

August 21

Dear Krystyna,

Dark thoughts haunt me more and more frequently. The tumor in my head doesn't give me any peace. I have been at the doctor's several times, but I still don't know the whole truth and I don't really have the time anymore to make further inquiry. I can find out more about the condition of my head by tapping it with my thumb than I can find out from the specialists.

I decided to write you a letter, because I don't want to bother my mother with additional problems anymore. A very strange sit-

uation has developed. The end of the novitiate is just a week away, and yet I am tormented by violent doubts. I am not sure that I will save my soul by treading this path. I don't feel that I have made even the most elementary principles of the inner life my own throughout all these months of my stay in the Order. My heart is filled with darkness, and my mind, like never before, is acting like a bowl of soft jelly. I don't know if I am dreaming or falling into an abyss.

There was a time when I believed that I was becoming more of a monk with every day, that I have many brothers in the Order of St. Paul the First Desert Hermit, who love me and care about me; that my father, whom I abandoned when I entered the novitiate, keeps appearing constantly by my side, shows an ever new face, changing his style of walking, his mimicry — he tenses his throat differently each time, when during Mass he sings "Dominus Vobiscum" or "Gloria in Excelsis Deo."

I believed that God for sure cared about me, since I made it all the way to this point, where every fellow human in the Order whom I call Father really is my father. But now I am starting to lose my way in His plans. It looks like He is releasing me from beneath His wings. I am falling like a stone. No one but myself comprehends the enormity of the depression that is overwhelming me. I now have a head made of cardboard, a wooden body fastened together with nails at the knees and elbows and a walking stick in my hand so I don't fall into a ditch.

I am just waiting now for the first light of dawn, which will knock out all the windows in the monastery and liberate my soul.

Dear Krysia, I ask for your prayers very much
Marcin

Epilogue

Mrs. Karolina Kowacz asked me to meet her shortly before she passed away. I knew her mainly from seeing her in passing. At one time, many years ago, we had lived on the same street. I was an altar boy then, and she the proud mother of a son who had entered the eremitic monastery of the Pauline Fathers on Jasna Góra. Her interest in me had its justification. I knew Brother Modest, her son, from the altar boys' circle that existed at the monastery. Attracted by his example I had also joined the Pauline Fathers. But we never met in the Order, even though I began my novitiate in the group right after his. He had died after an unsuccessful operation in Cracow, barely three months after taking his first vows.

I was very moved when Mrs. Kowacz, then already an elderly lady of 73, handed me the notes made by her son Marcin, who had the name Brother Modest in the novitiate. She knew that diary practically by heart. Up until now she had not dared share its content with anyone, but she finally came to the conclusion that she ought to show it to others. She chose me because I had followed the same path of monastic education as her son, I had the same Novice Master, and I walked the same meadows in Leśniów and the same fields of stubble. So I would be able to recognize many of the details and descriptions that found their way onto the pages of the diary. She had also read several of my articles in the press, which in her opinion could have been equally well written by her son. She was thoroughly convinced that Marcin had talent and a skillful pen, he had read a lot; too bad that Providence had taken him from this earth so early.

She had only one request: that I substitute new first and last names for the ones in the diary. Many of those people are still alive, and she did not want to offend anybody.

"I leave you a free hand in this matter," she decided.

Together with the four, rather dog-eared notebooks, she gave me a few photographs of Brother Modest in his white robe and a cardboard box of letters that was almost falling apart. It turned out that three years ago a neighbor's pipes on the floor above had cracked and water, flowing down the walls, had also gotten inside the little cabinet in which she kept Marcin's mementos. Mrs. Kowacz's younger son had immigrated to Canada, did not visit her very often, so it was very important to her that the notes not get lost.

I had not anticipated the many problems that cropped up with this matter. At first glance the material looked interesting. But deciphering it was sometimes beyond my ability. The notes were done by hand in pencil or ink, probably a ballpoint pen. Humidity and the water dripping from the pipes had done a lot of damage. Nonetheless I wanted to fulfill at all cost the commitment I had made. All the more so since Mrs. Kowacz died less than a year after our meeting and was buried next to her son at St. Roch Cemetery in Częstochowa.

Due to the laborious deciphering of the text and my own work as a practicing optician I didn't finish the transcription until many years later. In certain places, just like in restoring a beautiful fresco, I had to reconstruct whole sentences on the basis of three or four words, and even whole paragraphs. Since I had traveled the same path as the diary's author, it was easy for me to surmise or even complete the thought he had begun.

I must admit that I grew quite close to the work of the talented and prematurely deceased author. He charmed me with his sincerity, the higher flight of his mind and feelings, in comparison to those that accompany adolescents in similar situations who tread the monastic path. And if I could add my noble envy to the difficulty of struggling with the original, then, in an almost literal sense, I would want to identify myself with his texts and ascribe them more to myself than to the deceased, although without his respect for the written word this book would have never come to pass.

May the result of this intimate dialogue of twin minds, of doubled thoughts and viewpoints rendered aloud, be kindly appraised by a reader.

Tadeusz Chabrowski
New York, June 20, 2009

www.ingramcontent.com/pod-product-compliance
Lightning Source LLC
Chambersburg PA
CBHW071256250626
47159CB00004B/1214